With my
best regards

ONCE
THERE WAS A RAILROAD

Published by Peter's Press
Box 2112, Revelstoke
British Columbia, Canada, V0E 2S0

Phone: (250) 837•3558
E-mail: peter@revelstoke.net

National Library of Canada Cataloguing in Publication Data

Elkington, Peter W., 1923 –
    Once there was a railroad

    Includes bibliographical references.
    ISBN 0–9699944–5–1

1. Railroads—West (U.S.)—History—Fiction. 2. West
(U.S.)—History—Fiction. I. Title.
PS8559.L536O52 2001   C813'.54   C2001-910997-0
PR9199.3.E432O52 2001

CREDITS

All black and white photographs by the author

Copyediting
Wayne Magnuson, Prairie House Books, Calgary, Alberta

Interior and Cover Design
Jeremy Drought, Last Impression Publishing Service, Calgary, Alberta

Original Background Cover Photo
Milwaukee Road Steam Locomotive 261, ©1998 Tom Kelcec.

Printed and bound in Canada by Houghton Boston, Saskatoon, Saskatchewan

ONCE

THERE WAS A RAILROAD

THE STORY OF A DREAM

Peter W. Elkington

Revelstoke, British Columbia

DEDICATION

*To all those with a dream who knew
and worked for the gracious lady.*

• • •

*To my own true love, who urged me
to tell this story of a dream.*

CONTENTS

ACKNOWLEDGMENTS

I owe a debt of gratitude to Bill Wilkerson of Miles City, Montana, for sharing his memories with me. They were particularly valuable in recreating the story of the lines west. I have used his various monographs to flesh out the story of a dream. Judge Thomas H. Ploss's book *The Nation Pays Again* provided me with many insights into the management and mismanagement of a railroad. Professor Stanley Johnson's book *The Milwaukee Road Revisited* was a joy to read. It expressed the feelings of employees of the railroad and recalled the loving memories of a dream. Steve McCarter's *Guide to The Milwaukee Road in Montana* has served me well as a guide to the remaining vestiges and bones of a once-great railway.

To all those persons who were involved in the operations of the railroad, and to the kind and generous people of Montana for whom the railroad was an integral part of their life, who have kindly and freely given of their time and stories, I thank you. I am most grateful, for without you this book could not have been written.

My sincere thanks to the curators of the museums—for their time and helpful suggestions—which are listed on page 120.

My special thanks to Wayne Magnuson for his thoughtful comments and suggestions, and to Jeremy Drought for his cover design and typesetting of the book.

Photographs in the book are from the author's own collection.

FOREWORD

THE writing of this book was accidental. To me, as a small boy, railroads were enchanting because they took you to faraway places. I owned a model electric train with a bipolar engine, which traveled to exotic destinations. Trains of many colors, and engines with inspiring names, bedazzled my mind. I knew all the major eastern railways, and I had traveled on many of them. Of the western railways, I knew little. I had read about one electrified transcontinental railroad, but I had never seen it. It must have rivaled the *Pennsylvania Railroad*, which was electrified from New York to Washington.

It was many years later that I saw the transcontinental railroad. By then its magnificence was on the decline, and the electrified lines had been discontinued. On a trip to Montana, I saw one of the last freight trains ever to run from Chicago to Seattle. Soon most of that was gone. The abandoned right-of-way is there, but it too will vanish. Parts of the old roadbed have been taken over— converted to nature trails by the Forest Service; large sections have reverted to private hands, and are inaccessible to the public. Many sections have simply disintegrated over time. The tunnels, the trestles, and the bridges can still be seen. Some tunnels have been sold and are now used as places to grow mushrooms.

As I watched the demise of this famous railway, a story came to me, a story that needed to be written. Railroads are not just track and trains; they are people. It was the people's story that needed telling.

This is a work of fiction. But the railroad did exist, and the towns mentioned are real, although many are now ghost towns.

The people who energize the story are fictitious, but they live in my mind—and perhaps in the mind of the willing reader.

Peter W. Elkington
Revelstoke, BC
January 2001

Montana, The Treasure State

I have driven the length and breadth of Montana. It is a magical place. The sky and the land stretch to the far horizons. It is a land that has seen many migrations. The Cheyenne, the Crow, the Sioux, and the Blackfoot have ridden over the plains following the buffalo. West of the first mountain range, the Nez Perce and the Flatheads have called this land home. This is the land of Sacajawea, and Lewis and Clark, explorers who searched for an easy route to the Pacific, and who opened the way for adventurers, mountain men, entrepreneurs and homesteaders.

This is a land of vast expanses, of rolling grasslands and shimmering mountains. There is a grandeur to this land. It is a land of romance, hardship and heartbreak, a land of bitterly cold winters and crackling hot summers. Many people have come and gone, all attempting to put down roots and make a living, some prospering, some failing.

In the east, two major rivers cross the state. The Yellowstone and the Missouri flow from the mountains to join the Mississippi. Except for clusters of cottonwoods along their banks, they cross an area that is treeless and dry. This is ranching and agricultural country, dotted with small towns and large ranches.

The continental divide runs from north to south, separating Montana into two distinct parts and two contrasting lifestyles. The western area has snow-capped mountains and misty valleys, with narrow rivers flowing west. This is mining and lumber country, producing copper, gold and coal. The mountain slopes are covered with pines and hardwoods.

I found the best way to appreciate this beautiful country is to drive from east to west. The landscape gradually changes from the great grazing lands into more rolling, well-watered country. Here the trees begin, first a few pitiful specimens clinging to the hillsides and stream banks, then becoming more abundant as the land rises to meet the mountains. On the horizon is the rugged outline of the Rockies, distant and almost ghostly. The road ahead twists over the continental divide, through one of the many passes and down onto the great inland plateau. From there the rivers flow west toward the Pacific, plunging over falls and winding through canyons and valleys.

Across the state runs a scar, east to west. It comes out of the Dakotas and crosses the plains, finally snaking through the Bitterroot Mountains into Idaho. It is all that remains of a once-prosperous lifeline—a lifeline that supported many towns, settlements and ranches. Now the lifeline is gone, leaving those dependent on it struggling to survive. Some relied on new business and revenue. The buried remains of others are evidence of the toll, as are the solitary buildings, leaning sheds and deserted water towers. These mark the existence of once-thriving communities, now sad reminders of the fact that change is constant.

But in the end, the earth abides. So it is with Montana.

Once There Was A Railroad...

Once there was a railroad.
They made it run,
Made it race against time,
Now it's done.
Brother, can you spare a dime?

THIS is a romance, a story of true love and betrayal. It is the story of a railroad, of people and their dreams. Much of it could have happened, for the germ of the story is true. If you search for the places mentioned here, all you will find is a graveyard or two, a few dry bones, and some dilapidated buildings, through which the wind moans. The people are long gone. If you tarry in any one of these ghost towns and listen, you will hear whispers and voices of the past, and you might hear the lonely whistle of a steam locomotive as it approaches the station. The setting is Montana, from the rolling grasslands to the Rockies. A wealthy country, where fortunes were made and lost, but now an area largely deserted and forgotten.

I was following ghosts, which I often did. I followed the old right-of-way of the *Chicago, Madison, St. Paul & Pacific Railroad*, or what was left of it. In the little museum in Martinsdale, Montana, just up the street from the abandoned station, among other exhibits, I came across a packet of old letters tied with a faded blue ribbon. They were love letters. Some were tear stained, and some were crumpled, but all had been lovingly written, and lovingly kept. The curator allowed me to read them, and she told me that the museum had several more chests of letters and documents in the cellar, which I was welcome to peruse. Over the next few days I read a delightful, charming story of true love. One could only imagine the outcome: Who were these lovers, where had they come from and, of course, where had they gone? The curator could shed little light on the topic, except to say that the letters and documents had been part of an estate that had been willed to the museum a number of years before.

She told a strange tale of how, one day, a *UPS* delivery truck had deposited two large steamer trunks and several big crates at the museum. A letter from the law firm of Bedford, Sharpe, and Ringling in Chicago simply stated that this was the last bequest of the Ringling-O'Connor estate. The museum tried to contact the law firm. They received a stiff, formal reply informing them that these were the instructions of their late partner, George Ringling. The law firm also stated that they believed the documents had something to do with a railroad. The curator had no idea who the Ringlings or the O'Connors were and why they would bequeath these historical items and records to the museum. It intrigued the staff, for it was a mystery. The museum accepted the gift, put the valuable artifacts on exhibit, and stored the letters and documents. They had no way of tracing the estate. The only clue they had was the postmark on some of the old letters. This again was a dead end, for the town no longer existed and, according to the State Postal Authorities, there hadn't been such an office for many, many years.

The local historian told me about such a town, but no one lived there now. In fact, he didn't know precisely where it was; he had never been there. It had been a station of some importance on the old railroad—that much he knew. His directions were vague and uncertain. He suggested talking to the newspaper editor in the neighboring town.

The editor knew of the town. He and his mother had visited there several times when he was a youngster. It was a beautiful town, he remembered, with lots of flowers all up and down the street. As children, they had played hide-and-seek in the grove of great trees that surrounded the center square. At the end of the street, beyond the school, stood a big house with a magnificent garden. But now it was gone. He spoke of it with sadness, as though he was losing a precious memory.

I drove up the side road—a dirt road, overgrown, rutted, and obviously little used. An old railway right-of-way crossed the road, and just ahead there was a grove of ancient cottonwoods. Here and there among those giant trees were half-filled cellar holes, and nearby the remains of an abandoned church and a walled graveyard. On a little rise stood a ruined brick schoolhouse, its roof collapsed. One of its blackboards was intact, and through open windows I could make out a faded message written in chalk: *Enjoy your summer!*

The road past the school led to another rise, where substantial foundations and charred beams revealed that a sizable house had burned down—a tall, proud house that once looked out over the valley and town. Flowers still bloomed in profusion in the old garden and up and down the street, partially hiding the cellar holes and ruins. It had been a thriving town.

I looked at the half-ruined church, its bell and windows gone and most of the slats missing from the roof. I pushed aside the main door, which hung at a crazy angle, and entered the vestibule. It was empty and bare. Stairs led up to a dusty loft, but the organ and choir stalls were missing. Pigeons roosting in the old belfry burst though an opening in the roof and into the summer sky.

Over the main door was a carved staff with faint letters saying *Jacob's staff.* I walked down the nave, past the two remaining pews, which were cracked and falling apart. I could still read the faint inscription on the wall above the place where the altar once stood:

The church of St. Jude, the Obscure,
the patron saint of dreamers.

That was all that remained, except for the walled graveyard outside.

The abandoned railway right-of-way followed the winding river. Down by the old trainyard a collapsing freight shed still bore the name of the town on one of its walls. The golden letters were pealing, but the name was clear:

MONARCH

I stood in the old town square watching a flock of wild turkeys strut in the empty dooryards and scratch in the overgrown gardens. Rabbits hopped around the ancient tree trunks. A dogfox barked in a nearby field. A soft breeze stirred the cottonwood leaves. Then all was still. Nature had reclaimed Monarch.

I drove to Forsyth, the county seat. The County Historical Society had a wealth of pictures of Monarch in their collection: pictures of celebrations in the town square and the arrival of special trains. It had been a busy, happy town. I was told that because of its size and importance Monarch had once been considered for the county seat of Primrose County—the sheep and cattle ranching center. More sheep, wool and cattle had been shipped from Monarch than from any other town in the state. One picture, of a large mansion surrounded by a well-tended flower and vegetable garden, was the home of a family of very wealthy ranchers, the Ashmeads. The day after the railroad had ceased operations, the house had mysteriously burned down. With the death of the railway, the people had moved away, leaving only memories, ghosts and flowers.

It was in Monarch that I found the beginnings of my story.

THE CHICAGO, MADISON,
ST. PAUL & PACIFIC

I wandered along the old abandoned roadbed, past dilapidated, tumbled-down depots; past deserted generating stations and dismantled water towers. I walked through tunnels and over trestles and bridges, looking for some sign, some indication, of what had really been here. Near an old unpainted station I found a railway spike, but that was all. I stood on an overpass looking down the abandoned right-of-way that soon narrowed and became a line in the distance. If I listened carefully I could hear, faint on the wind, the air horn of a *Little Joe* or the rumble of a freight train.

The heart of a great railroad had been ripped out, its body violated. Ghosts still haunted the area. Questions flooded my mind. How had a once-proud, prosperous and progressive railway, over 150 years old, fallen from grace, so that only bits and pieces of evidence remained? I believe the answers are buried with the railway and the people connected with it.

• • •

The story seems to divide with the railway. The eastern division has almost disappeared in the urban sprawl, or has been sold piecemeal to competitors. Only a few stately stations remain, as neglected as elderly maiden aunts fallen on hard times. In the western division, or the lines west, the skeleton and a few bones are still visible. I was standing beside one of its old depots. The brick platform had been torn up and sold for salvage. From the Missouri River to the Pacific Ocean the destruction had been mindless, violent, and total.

To me, this was tragic. What happened to the people who labored so lovingly on the railroad? What of the little towns so dependent on the railway? What of the economy of the countryside? Of farmers and ranchers who transported their bounty to market by rail? In my search for answers I found people who still mourn the passing of the railway. I found ghost towns and deserted ranches, once prosperous, now rotting slowly away.

Here was a beautiful, sad story of heartbreak and tragedy—of life and death. The *Chicago, Madison, St. Paul, & Pacific Railroad* enjoyed fame and fortune, yet was betrayed by an uncaring, greedy management. A management without vision that, in the end, systematically destroyed the railroad and left it to perish in the dust.

• • •

The *St. Paul Railroad* began humbly enough, hauling farm produce to the Chicago market. Over the years it expanded into five states. It was a prosperous and profitable railway, connected with the powerful *Union Pacific* at Omaha and the *Santa Fe* in St. Louis. What it lacked was a direct connection to the Pacific Northwest. There were two northern railroads, but they didn't come into Chicago. In the late 1890s it was decided to extend the *St. Paul* to the Pacific through states not served by other routes:

up through Wisconsin, across the Missouri river, on through South Dakota, Montana, over the mountains into Idaho, and finally into Washington state. By the early twentieth century the line was complete. The *Chicago, Madison, St. Paul, & Pacific* was truly a transcontinental railway. There was plenty of traffic, more than enough for the three northern railroads.

A vigorous advertising campaign was launched extolling the bounties of the west. Ranches, farms, and small towns were established in the fertile grasslands. Mining communities boomed as the great copper deposits of the inland plateau were exploited. The *St. Paul* ran freight and passenger service direct from Chicago to the west coast, something its rivals could not do. It was a bold and imaginative railroad, always interested in innovations that were both profitable and far-reaching. Within five years after the completion of the transcontinental line, the Rocky Mountain and Pacific Coast divisions were electrified.

I wandered about the district, picking up bits and pieces, following insubstantial leads and reading old records, newspapers and letters. Along the way, there were many ex-employees who told their stories, who made suggestions of sites to be visited and provided other leads to follow.

From all my notes and research I developed a tale which revolved around a town, seven strong-minded people, all dreamers with a vision, and a railway. It became the story of the town of Monarch, the twins William and George Ashmead, George's wife Mary, old Jacob August Armour, Amy Ashmead and her two husbands (Rob Ringling and Michael O'Connor) and the *Chicago, Madison, St. Paul, & Pacific Railroad.*

GEORGE ASHMEAD

I left Monarch and drove to Helena, the state capital. In the archives of the State Historical Society there would be records or accounts of the town. The curator was a great help and gave me access to the dusty records of Monarch and surrounding countryside. I sat at the table trying to piece together evidence of the cattle and sheep ranches that had flourished in eastern Montana. I was surrounded by paper, bills, documents, letters, and contracts and, at the bottom of the heap, old journals. One journal, *The Ashmead Ranch and Cattle Company,* told how George and Mary Ashmead had founded the company in the late nineteenth century, soon becoming a prominent, prosperous operation. After World War II it had been bought and merged into a larger, more affluent cattle company. Now all that remained were the fields where cattle and sheep had grazed. Of the town, nothing remained. George Ashmead's journal was a story of a dream.

• • •

George Ashmead was six feet tall and of wiry build. He had light sandy hair and blue eyes, a very handsome young man who walked with an air of confidence. He and his twin brother, William, had recently been discharged from the Union Army.

They'd had enough of war, misery, and killing. Having received their final bonus pay, they planned to go west to seek their fortunes. Although the family home was still in Chicago, both of their parents had died. William was fascinated with railroads, and George was looking for ranchland. He believed that cattle and sheep were the key to the future. He was looking for the best ranchland he could find.

He left his brother in Fargo and boarded the train for Bismarck in the Dakota Territory. The ride was long, hot, dirty, and uncomfortable. Soot and cinders came in through the open coach windows covering everything with grime. George saw nothing that impressed him, only endless rolling grasslands. There was little water, and very few trees. As he sat looking out the coach window he thought he saw a figure on horseback in the distance, but he was never quite sure.

The train stopped with a jolt, throwing George headfirst into the seat in front of him. He got up, rubbed his head, picked up his hat, and walked to the front of the car. From horizon to horizon he saw buffalo, a huge seething mass plodding slowly across the track. There were thousands of them, with no end in sight. George walked to the front of the engine and climbed up on the cowcatcher, joining several other passengers also watching the herd. When it got too hot sitting there in the afternoon sunshine, he climbed down. The train sat on the track, huffing and puffing, as if impatient to be off. The engineer and fireman lay in the shade of the engine, napping. There was nothing to do but wait.

Some of the passengers slept in the shade afforded by the passenger cars, some played cards, and some walked back down the track. George and the conductor sat together discussing land and its availability. After what seemed like hours, the herd moved on. The engineer blew the whistle, all the passengers climbed back on board and the train moved on. It was night when they reached Bismarck, a small, busy trading town on the banks of the Missouri River.

George walked across the street to a small hotel. The innkeeper gave him a towel and pointed to the pump in the backyard. George washed as best he could, then went in for supper. The evening meal was served family style on long trestle tables covered with red and white checkered tablecloths. Bowls of hot, steaming meat and vegetables were placed on the table, and everyone helped themselves. That night George shared a dormitory room with five others.

The innkeeper was a great one for visiting. Over a breakfast of ham, fried eggs, hash-brown potatoes and hot coffee, the innkeeper asked, "Say, young man, where are you off to? There ain't much further on, you know."

"I'm looking for ranchland," George replied.

"What do you want to go out there for? Ain't nothing but wild savage Indians."

"Well, I'm going to go look anyway."

"Good luck, young fella. You won't find much."

George finished his breakfast, paid his bill, picked up his bag, crossed the street and boarded the waiting train. On the bluffs across the river were the ruins of the great Mandan settlement, which had been wiped out by smallpox half a century earlier. The train gave a shrill whistle and steamed slowly out of the station. After crossing the shaky wooden bridge over the Missouri River, it rolled out onto the great, wide-open, grassy plains. During the day George again thought he saw men on horseback in the distance but they were too far away to be sure, just silhouettes on the hills. The plains seemed empty, endless. Now and then they passed small herds of pronghorn antelope grazing peacefully beside the track.

After another long, hot day's ride they crossed the Yellowstone River and stopped at Forsyth. It wasn't much of a town, barely a handful of houses, a small inn, a few stores, a post office and a saloon. It was the railroad construction depot, with its dormitories, supply shacks, and construction sheds. Track construction ended just a few miles further west. All along the right-of-way were piles of ties, steel track and other equipment. At the edge of town was the encampment of the US 7th Cavalry, there to protect the railroad and its construction crews from marauding Indians. Their commander, a flamboyant young general named Custer, would come into town and brag that he and his men could subdue these savages at any time. George listened to all this, but paid little attention. Subduing the Indians was not as easy as Custer made out, for the Northern Cheyenne and Sioux had other ideas. The prairies was their homeland, and the buffalo their source of food and clothing. What did these white men know of the Great Spirit and the land?

After surveying the available land for sale, George went back to Minneapolis a little discouraged. He had not found land that suited him. Most of it was too dry, or poorly surveyed.

In 1873–74 the United States suffered a major economic depression that devastated many businesses and destroyed the native populations in the West. Both northern transcontinental railroads declared bankruptcy, and all construction work stopped. The US Army, on orders from the federal government, began a systematic slaughter of the buffalo, thus depriving the Indians of the their livelihood and food supply. The winter of 1874 was particularly severe. There was widespread starvation among the western Indian tribes. The egotistical commander of the 7th Cavalry boasted that he was responsible for the subjugation of the local Indians. He and the 7th Cavalry marched out for a final victory, only to be ambushed and wiped out by the Northern Cheyenne and Sioux under the command of the great Sioux chief Sitting Bull.

The Crow nation remained neutral and had stayed on sidelines, much to the rage of the other tribes. The wise old Crow chief had a vision in which he saw fields of spotted buffalo, and had been told in a dream that education of his people in the ways of the white man, was they way to peace.

The Crow were to follow the ways of cooperation and education rather than confrontation and conflict, and they fared better than many of the other tribes.

The next spring George set out again. This time with detailed land surveys and maps. There was cheap land to be had in the Montana Territory. He got down from the train at the little town of Hysham, the next station west of Forsyth. Hysham had one street that paralleled the tracks, and a few scattered houses. Across the street from the station was a bar and hotel, a store with a post office, a bank, a corral and livery stable, and a rickety building that seemed to lean against the bank for protection. This was the railway land office.

The *Northern Pacific Railroad* had been given federal land grants along their right-of-way, which they sold to homesteaders and would-be ranchers. George bought a whole section of land that bordered the Yellowstone River in the south and stretched north to the banks of the Musselshell River. The section was made up of rolling grasslands, well watered, and well suited for cattle and sheep ranching. He purchased a pair of horses from the local livery stable, and equipment at the general store. He packed his gear, loaded it on his horses and went down to the riverbank. There he boarded the cable ferry that took him across the Yellowstone River. It was a small ferry, just enough room for a wagon and a team of horses. Once across, he rode north to survey his land. It was to be the basis for his inland ranching empire. He rode up the trail, leading his packhorse over the dry grasslands. He was pleased with what he found, but he couldn't see a location for a town. He stopped at several likely places, but none of them seemed right. Discouraged, he turned his horses back toward Hysham.

That night he made camp by a stream, his horses tethered nearby. He sat by the fire writing in his journal, now and then pausing to listen to the night noises. Hearing a slight noise he looked up, and standing on the opposite side of the fire was a young Crow warrior. His approach had been absolutely silent.

The young warrior was tall and lean. He wore buckskin leggings and beaded moccasins. Around his shoulder was a multicolored blanket. He had a single eagle feather in his jet-black hair. Over his arm was a rifle. George was surprised, for in all his travels he hadn't seen a soul. He raised his hand in peace. The warrior nodded, sat down and took out his pipe. They sat in a peaceful silence and smoked the pipe. At last the Crow warrior, in halting English, asked George what he had been doing. He had watched George for several days as he rode over the land. George explained his purpose. They talked of many things, and of George's dream of a cattle ranch. The Indian nodded, smoked. These were the spotted buffalo the great Crow chief had dreamed about. George went on to speak of his desire for a townsite, where people could live together in peace. At last the warrior rose, put his pipe away, wrapped his blanket around his shoulders and said, "Peace. I will be back in the morning," and vanished into the night.

In the morning George ate his breakfast, packed his saddlebags, loaded up his packhorse, mounted his own horse and started back toward Hysham. There was no sign of the young warrior. George was disappointed, for he was looking forward to seeing him again. George rode up a small rise and looked out over the land, and it pleased him. Then he turned and headed back along the trail to town. When he rounded a bend, there was the young warrior, mounted and waiting for him. They saluted each other. The warrior turned his horse and beckoned George to follow. Leaving the main trail they followed a faint path that wandered over the rolling grasslands. They rode most of the morning. It was a pleasant day, with a warm, gentle breeze making waves in the grass. In the early afternoon they arrived at a pretty hollow by a small river. It was a peaceful place, with a grove of cottonwood trees standing in a circle at the center. Here was George's town site. The Indian warrior raised his arm and saluted, then turned his horse and rode away.

George made camp within the circle of cottonwoods. He sat by the fire listening to the wind whisper through the leaves. They seemed to speak of greatness and joy, and to whisper a name, which George couldn't quite catch. He took out his journal and sketched out the plan for his town, with the grove of trees as central square. The townsite was located in the middle of his land, and so he marked it on his map. It would be a beautiful town, full of flowers. Its main street would circle the trees. He would build his house on a small rise overlooking the valley. The other end of the street would connect with the main trail. It had been a lovely day and George was happy. He climbed into his bedroll and slept soundly and peacefully. In the middle of the night he awoke, the town's name having sprung to mind. He would call the town Monarch, for its location seemed to command the surrounding territory.

In the morning George packed the horses and headed down the trail to Hysham. Dreams of *The Ashmead Ranch and Cattle Company*, headquartered in Monarch, danced through his head. He stopped in Hysham long enough to sell his horses and store his equipment. Then he registered his land title with the railway land office and deposited some of his maps and surveys in the bank. With the land title, a map of the land and a sketch of Monarch safely in his pocket, he caught the train for Minneapolis.

Arriving safely back in Chicago, he rushed off to see his high-school sweetheart, the pretty, young Mary Armour. They sat together in the parlor of the Armour mansion, pouring over George's plans. George proposed to Mary, but Mary told him to come back the next day and ask her father's permission. George kissed Mary good night and left in a very happy mood.

The next day, dressed in his best suit, he paid a formal call on old Jacob Armour. The session was stormy and short. Jacob thought George was a dreamer with no prospects, and told him to forget about Mary. As he left, Mary stopped him and pulled him into the parlor. "Bring all your maps and plans tomorrow," she whispered. "Be firm in your dream, and this will convince father." Then she looked lovingly into his eyes and kissed him.

The following day George returned with all his plans and maps. His session with Jacob was again heated and stormy, but George noticed a weakening in the old man's attitude and he knew Mary was listening at the keyhole. Jacob snorted and suddenly stormed out of the room, knocking Mary over as he opened the door. After picking her up he took her back into the study. She and George flew into each other's arms. Old Jacob growled and sputtered. He opened the door and called to Mary's mother. Catharine Armour came in, looked at George and Mary, and smiled. She walked over, embraced her husband and kissed him, then whispered in his ear. There was no more to be said. George and Mary were married shortly after that momentous day.

George returned Monarch. Two months later, when he had finished building a house on the rise, he sent for Mary. One evening they stood on the knoll holding hands and looking over the townsite. This was home! George leaned down and kissed Mary full on the lips. Mary was equally passionate in her response. George and Mary had found their dream.

JACOB A. ARMOUR

I sat in my garden holding the beautifully carved staff that I'd found in the ruins of the church at Monarch. It felt warm, and pleasing to the touch. The staff seemed to have a life of its own. It had been fashioned well, by skillful hands. There were two sets of initials, one at each end. Who were *J.A.A.* and *C.S.A.*? I had seen the staff above the door in the old church with its faint inscription, *Jacob's Staff*. I hadn't thought much about it when I was in the church. Who was Jacob? How was he connected with Monarch? The staff seemed to speak to me. Later that week when I was reading back copies of the *Chicago Daily Tribune*, I found a clue. On the society page was the account of the wedding of George Ashmead of Monarch, Montana, and Mary Catharine Armour, daughter of Jacob A. and Catharine S. Armour, of Chicago. Here was the connection.

• • •

It was a beautiful day. Young Jacob sat under a tree, the valley spread out below him. He whistled softly to himself, Bach's *Sheep May Safely Graze*, an air he had heard in church. He carved diligently on an oddly-shaped knot of wood. The Armours were sturdy members of the farm community. Young Jacob Armour was the last of his brothers and sisters to remain at home. He had no desire to be a farmer or work the land, but he had a great ambition to be wealthy, and dreamed of making a fortune. His father had apprenticed him to the local butcher, a large, fat, red-faced man with a vile temper. Jacob hated working for him, although he *was* learning the butcher's trade. On his days off he would wander over the hills or sit and dream.

Now he sat under a tree on the hillside, carving an intricate design on the beautiful knot of wood that he had found. It was a design of entwining vines and leaves. In the center he carved the initials of his love: *C.S.* Catharine was the pretty daughter of a prosperous merchant in the town. Herr Schultz was a firm believer in strong family traditions, where the father's word was law. Jacob loved Catharine and wanted to marry her, but her father was adamant, for how could Jacob support a wife when he had no prospects or trade? This hurt Jacob because he knew that someday he would be successful. True, Jacob was learning the meat-cutting business, he was skillful and certainly ambitious, but he was still an apprentice.

So he dreamed as he carved. He would go to the New World and make his fortune. He would show all the scoffers and doubters. He finished the carving, got up, brushed off his pants, put his knife in his pocket, ran his fingers through his unruly hair and started down the hill to the village. Halfway down the hill was a little roadside chapel, a place where lovers and dreamers came, and where travelers paused for a rest. It was dedicated to St. Jude, the patron saint of dreamers. Jacob often came here. This day he went in and sat in one of the pews, thinking, and dreaming of the future. Before he left he asked the Saint's blessing, for himself, his love, and the carving.

That evening, dressed in a clean shirt and pants, he called on Catharine. He gave her the carving and told her of his plans. She loved Jacob and believed in his dreams, but the New World was so far away that she wondered if she would ever see him again. Jacob promised to write every month, and that as soon as he had enough money he would come back for her. Catharine's father scoffed at the whole idea, and said that the young idiot was just dreaming and would never come back. But Herr Schultz did promise Catharine and Jacob that if Jacob came back in three years with enough money, they could get married. Catharine knew Jacob would return.

Much to Herr Schultz's surprise, for he never expected to see Jacob again, Jacob returned to his home village within the three years, and with a small fortune. Jacob had settled in Chicago and opened his own butcher shop, which had become very successful. Now he asked for Catharine's hand in marriage. Herr Schultz grumbled but gave his permission and they were married in the town church. Before they left for Chicago, Jacob and Catharine went to the little chapel on the hill and prayed for a blessing from St. Jude.

Jacob's butcher shop grew and prospered. He expanded from one store to several, then into the packing-house business. Chicago was expanding fast and boasted several large meat-packing plants. A hard-driving Jacob Armour ran the very prosperous *Armour and Company*, one of the biggest and most successful packing houses in the city. Its reputation was made when he negotiated a government contract to supply meat to the Union Army.

Jacob was a short, heavy-set man, and in his later years, tended to be overweight. He had small very bright eyes and close-cropped, gray hair. His flowered waistcoat was held together across his ample belly by a large gold chain. His business had grown and expanded with his girth. By the early seventies *Armour and Company* was the most profitable of the city's packing houses.

Jacob bought cattle and sheep in the west, and had them shipped to Chicago by rail. The finished meat products were then shipped on to the east coast markets.

Jacob and Catharine had a large family of lively children. He loved them all dearly. His youngest daughter, Mary, was the apple of his eye. Young George Ashmead had fallen in love with Mary, and Mary with George. They had known each other from their school days, before the war. During the war, George and Mary had kept up a lively correspondence. The war now over, George presented himself to old Jacob to ask for Mary's hand in marriage.

"Sir, I wish to marry your daughter Mary."

"Outrageous! What prospects do you have, young man?" Jacob growled, remembering his own father-in-law's resistance.

"I own a full section of land in the Montana Territory, and I plan to raise sheep and cattle there."

"You expect my daughter to live in the wilds of Montana with all those savage Indians. You're crazy. Get out of here!"

Without so much as a goodbye, old Jacob showed George the door. He considered George an upstart and a dreamer. George left the house. Jacob sat in his study. The boy had charm and he wasn't afraid to dream. Jacob thought of his own youth when he, too, sat in the wayside chapel of St. Jude and dreamed dreams. Perhaps he should think again. That evening as he and his beloved Catharine sat by the fire, they had a long discussion about Mary and George, and about dreams.

The next day when George returned, he had plans, maps, and drawings of Monarch. The meeting with Jacob was as stormy and loud as the day before. To Jacob, who would hardly look at the plans, marriage to Mary was still out of the question. George's ideas were just too wild. Who in their right mind would want to leave Chicago and live in the wild west, populated by savages and wild animals? Jacob, still furious, stormed out of the room knocking over his dear Mary, who had been listening at the keyhole. Jacob picked her up and said, "Well, Missy, as long as you have been spying on us and listening at the door, you might as well come in and tell this fool of a boy where to go."

He grabbed Mary by the hand and pulled her back into the study. Mary rushed into George's arms and held him close. Jacob growled, went to the study door and called Catharine. She could make these young people listen to reason.

Catharine was working in the parlor when she heard Jacob call. She came into the study, looked at George and Mary, and smiled. Then she walked over and embraced and kissed her husband. Soothingly she whispered in his ear, "Ach liebchen. Isn't it wonderful that our Mary has found herself a man? And she loves him, too. Young George is such a nice boy, nicht?"

Jacob scowled and grumbled and rumbled like a spent thunderstorm. The discussion went back and forth between all four, but in the end, Jacob reluctantly agreed.

It was a grand wedding, and after the honeymoon, George left for Monarch to build a house near the ancient grove of trees.

Two months later a letter arrived, with train fare, saying the house was ready and Mary should come. Jacob said he was coming too. Not so much to protect his daughter, but to see for himself the wild schemes this crazy boy had in mind. Catharine said she would visit later, when the town was fully established.

George met the train at Forsyth. Jacob was dirty, tired and grumpy, but Mary was alive and eager with excitement. George had made reservations for them at the best hotel. After a hot bath and an excellent supper, Jacob was feeling much better. The next morning, a breakfast of antelope sausage, eggs, and pancakes put old Jacob in an expansive mood. It was a half a day's trip to

Monarch, and Jacob was quite taken with the wide-open spaces and the endless sky. He could see great possibilities for cattle and sheep ranches. He agreed to bankroll *The Ashmead Ranch and Cattle Company*. However, he made one proviso for his support: *Armour and Company* were to have first bid on all cattle and sheep shipped to Chicago.

Mary was enchanted with Monarch. She and George walked all over the townsite, planning a building here and a building there. After breakfast one day, she and George took the buckboard and drove to the far reaches of the ranch. Old Jacob finished his coffee, got up from the kitchen table, set his hat square on his head, picked up his walking cane and went out the door. He walked down by the river and back up along the main trail. He paused to pick up a nice looking branch that caught his fancy and walked on. He sat down under one of the great trees, took off his hat and wiped his face and head. It was a warm day and he was sweating profusely. He reached into his pocket for his favorite knife and began to whittle the branch. He shaped it, smoothed it, and without thinking he carved a simple design of twisting vines and leaves. As he did so he quietly whistled to himself, the same Bach air he had whistled so long ago. When it was finished he looked at it, smiled to himself, then carved the initials *J. A. A.* and the date at the end of the staff. It was just the right size and weight. It had balance, and it felt right in the hand. He sat there holding the staff. He hadn't realized what he had carved. It had just come to him, like the Bach air he had whistled. He remembered how he had carved the wooden knot years ago, of entwining vines and leaves, and in the middle the initials of his beloved. He thought of her now, and of how much he loved her, and wished she was with him. He took out his knife again and carved the initials *C.S.A.* at the other end of the staff.

Then he got up, put his knife back in his pocket, wiped his face, put on his hat and continued walking around the circle of trees, carrying his new staff. He was curious about this town. George and Mary were so enthusiastic that Jacob was just a little suspicious. Again he walked around the circle of trees. Half way around he came to a nice level area and stopped, He stood there for a long time, holding his staff. He thought again of his dear wife in Chicago. He thought of George and Mary and their future. His wife's voice came to him. He suddenly jammed his new staff into the ground, and growled, "That's where the church will be. We'll build it. And it will be dedicated to St. Jude, the Obscure, the patron saint of all those who dare to dream."

Pleased with the idea he walked back to the house, smiling to himself. He clasped his hands behind his back, and put his walking stick under his arm. When he reached the front porch he sat in the rocking chair, fanning himself with his hat, as he remembered the blessings of St. Jude and the little chapel on the hillside. When George and Mary returned, they all walked over to the church site—Jacob's church. Monarch would be a beautiful town. When the town was finished, Jacob said to himself he must bring his beloved wife for a visit, but he never did.

WILLIAM ASHMEAD

I sat in the archives of the *Chicago Historical Society* searching through musty old records and papers dealing with the great railroad expansion in the eighties and nineties. Dust motes danced in the sunlight that streamed through the dirty window. Railroads had spread out from the city in all directions. There were a number of profitable granger lines, built to provide transportation of farm produce to local markets. In a battered box, stuffed on a back shelf, I found records of a forgotten railway, and the journal of William Ashmead.

William Ashmead was a dreamer, a planner, and a pioneer. I began reading this strange story, and became so engrossed that I lost all sense of time. A knock on the door roused me. The night janitor stood there.

"You planning to stay all night?"

"Well no, I didn't realize how late it was."

I put the journal back in the box of papers, picked up my hat and coat and went out the door. The janitor followed me out to the street and said, "Good night to you, sir. We'll see you in the morning." Then he turned, re-entered the building and locked the main door.

• • •

After William Ashmead and his twin brother George had been discharged from the Union Army, they traveled west. They made a striking pair—both tall, blond and very handsome. William was fascinated by railroads. He had seen what they could do during the war. Now he dreamed on a larger scale. In Minneapolis there lived another dreamer, the one-eyed Canadian, James J. Hill, who was in the process of building a railroad west from St. Paul to Seattle on the Pacific Coast. It would run just south of the Canadian border, and compete with the *Canadian Pacific.* Hill believed that prosperity of the country was based on trade, particularly Pacific trade. William made an appointment to see James J. Hill.

William found Hill in an old warehouse near the tracks. He was ushered into an upstairs office overlooking the railyards. After the usual introductions, they sat together, the grizzled old veteran of the Canadian rail wars and the handsome young war veteran, pouring over maps and plans. The table was littered with paper. They discussed many possibilities, all dealing with railroads. Hill liked William's ideas on trade and transport. The young man had a head on his shoulders. At the end of the interview, which had lasted two hours, Hill hired William to do all the little odd jobs that he didn't like to do himself.

Several months later, as William was reading an inventory report, Hill stopped by his desk. "William, you've done well," he said. "You're a good man with good ideas, and you work hard. I've been watching you. I need a track boss. Would you like to work in the field for a year or so?" He didn't wait for an answer. "This year the track has to be laid across the Dakotas before winter comes, without fail. I need a supervisor to see that the work is done properly. I think you can do it. And William, remember, go where the money is being spent."

William agreed and was soon organizing surveyors, suppliers, and track crews. The operation began in Grand Forks on the Red River, and as the last of the snow melted, the crews headed west. Mile after mile of track was laid over the grassy plains. The track crews were rotated, one day on, one day off, from dawn to dusk, six days a week. James J. Hill had ruled that there was to be no work on Sundays. At the end of each day, ties, track, and barrels of spikes, plus other equipment, were brought to the railhead for the next day's crew. Every morning William, dressed in overalls, work boots, and a battered hat to shade his head, was at the railhead when the day's work began. The crew that laid the most miles of track in a day earned a substantial bonus. Every morning the track foreman greeted him with a cheery "Good Morning, William. Today is *our* day. Off we go boys!"

Much to Hill's surprise, the track reached Williston on the Missouri before the first snowfall. There, all equipment was stored for the winter. Shelby, Montana, was to be next year's goal. This section would take longer, as the countryside was more rolling than flat. When the work was finished and the equipment had been stored, William rode the work train back to St. Paul.

Next morning, William, dressed in new clean clothes, sat in Hill's cluttered office. Maps were spread out on the conference table. They discussed the summer's work.

"You did better than I thought, William," growled Hill. "The Superintendent needs a new assistant. Do you think you can handle the job? I think you can. Your next project is to find and survey a suitable pass over the continental divide. There must be one."

"Thank you, sir," William replied. "I'm glad you have confidence in my work."

The next year the survey work began as soon as they could travel in the mountains. William went ahead, trekking over faint

Indian trails and marking possible routes. The crews surveyed through the Blackfoot Reservation into the mountains, over the continental divide through Marias Pass, and down the other side to Columbia Falls. It was the lowest pass south of the Canadian border, a difficult climb for long trains, but it was the only feasible route. The right-of-way was surveyed from Shelby to Columbia Falls. Spring came and the track crew began laying track from Williston to Shelby. Perhaps they could reach Browning by winter. The following year the tracks would be laid right up through the pass. Such was the plan.

1873 was a disastrous year. North America sank into a deep depression. Factories and businesses closed, all major construction, including railroads, ground to a halt. Thousands of men were laid off. Business blamed the government, the government blamed the banks, and the workers blamed everybody, including the president. The government seemed helpless in the face of this misery. In the cities there were soup kitchens and bread lines. The railroads virtually stopped running, and construction, including all major track-laying operations, ceased. As workers were laid off, they just dropped their tools, stacked their equipment and left.

Farmers who relied on the short granger railroads around Chicago had difficulty getting their produce to market, and, even if they did, prices were ridiculously low: three dollars for a boxcar full of melons. The banks foreclosed on farm mortgages and called in industrial loans, leaving industry and agriculture scrambling. The two northern railroads declared bankruptcy, abandoned all construction, and left their stock piles of equipment all along the abandoned right-of-way.

William was paid off; there was no more work. He returned to Chicago disheartened, for this seemed to be the end of a promising railroad career. James J. Hill sailed for Europe to attract new investors and new money for his *Great Northern Railroad*. Hill's great rival, Henry Villard, of the *Northern Pacific*, was in Germany, but he was not so successful in attracting new money.

Running out of Chicago was a very prosperous granger railroad—*The Chicago, Madison & St. Paul*—a bright, sparkling railroad. Its lines reached into five states and it had survived the depression better than most. It served the surrounding countryside efficiently and well. The president of the *St. Paul Railroad* suffered an unexpected heart attack and died. The board of directors began searching for a young, energetic, forward-looking man to replace him. On the recommendation of James J. Hill, William Ashmead was chosen as the new president of the *St. Paul*. His first priority was to improve the rolling stock and to lay heavier track. For, as he told his board of directors, you can't earn money with worn-out equipment. For the next twenty years the *St. Paul* paid handsome dividends to its stockholders.

William had a dream for his railroad, a dream to extend it to the Pacific Coast, much as James J. Hill wanted to do with the *Great Northern*. There were large empty sections of North and South Dakota, Montana, Idaho, and Washington not served by either of the northern railroads. Hill's *Great Northern Railroad* ran too far north, too close to the Canadian border, and Villard's *Northern Pacific* didn't serve Chicago. Its main terminal was Duluth on Lake Superior. The *St. Paul* had a terminal at La Cross on the Mississippi. William planed to extend the *St. Paul* to Mobridge on the Missouri. The board of directors agreed on the expansion, but wanted to allow a few years before the next new extension. This way, the line would pay for the expansion through revenues.

The expansion continued, and each extension proved very profitable. After Mobridge on the Missouri, it was Miles City on the Yellowstone. Surveys had been made along the Musselshell valley passing through Monarch and the rich ranchlands of eastern Montana; then to Three Forks, the headwaters of the Missouri, over the continental divide through Pipestone Pass to the great interior plateau of Montana, and the copper-mining communities of Butte and Anaconda. The survey continued along Clarks Fork River, up over the Bitterroot Mountains, then down the pacific slope to Portland and Tacoma. There were tunnels, trestles, and bridges to build. Nowhere along the line was the grade to be greater than two percent. The *St. Paul* was on its way.

In Chicago, William built a reputation for being a very astute, aggressive and competent businessman. He was well respected by all levels of society. He cut a dashing figure, always immaculately dressed, among Chicago's elite. The young ladies of the city competed with each other to invite this handsome bachelor to their balls, supper parties, or private soirees. William was flattered, but his fancy fell upon the young and very beautiful Victoria Spalding. The Spaldings were wealthy grain merchants, who lived on the north side of Chicago. James Spalding, Victoria's father, knew William through their business dealings, and respected him. Every summer the Spaldings migrated to their 20-room cottage on Lake Geneva in order to escape the city heat. William was often invited for a weekend of tennis.

The beautiful Victoria, the Spaldings' second daughter, was a vain young lady. She wore only the latest fashions. Her blond hair was styled to enhance her peaches-and-cream complexion. She had large, china-blue eyes, which gave her the look of sweet innocence. She set her cap for the dashing William, and William was smitten by her beauty and charm. After a suitable engagement of one year, they were married. Their wedding, in Chicago's Episcopal Cathedral, was the social highlight of the year. Shortly after their

An abandoned station at Martinsdale, MT.

The circle of trees, as seen from the road to Monarch, MT.

A trestle with gantry for overhead wires, near Saltese, MT.

A viaduct with the center section removed, near Soudan, MT.

Missoula Station, Missoula, MT.

Vandalized power generating station at Loweth, MT.

Butte Station, Butte, MT.

Platform at Butte Station, Butte MT.

The Montana Hotel in Alberton, MT.

Three Forks Station, Three Forks, MT.

honeymoon William recognized Victoria's limitations. She was very sweet and kind, but had no interest whatever in the railroad, or any other commercial business. Her main interests were clothes, high fashion, and Chicago society, and William could pay.

Victoria held an open house for tea and gossip for her friends every Thursday. The other days of week she went to other open houses of the society's elite. She had little dinner parties for her friends, whom William didn't particularly like, but whom he tolerated for Victoria's sake. They lived separate lives, meeting at dinner each night to exchange the happenings of the day. They didn't dislike each other; in fact they rather liked this type of platonic companionship, for it had its advantages, but they had nothing in common. Victoria spent her days shopping and attending afternoon tea parties, where local gossip was exchanged. She related this gossip to William over dinner, and he listened very carefully. He in turn told of people he had met that day. Victoria didn't realize what she was doing, but William valued the gossip, for he used this information against his competitors. After dinner they retired to the parlor or the library, where coffee was served. William read the evening paper and smoked his daily cigar, and Victoria tatted or crocheted some small object, or she might play the piano.

With the expansion of the *St. Paul*, William was on the road a great deal. He always remembered to bring some precious or unusual gift back to delight Victoria. In railroad building, he followed James J. Hill's maxim: you go where the money is being spent. It was a great day when he followed the tracklayers into Monarch, which had grown as the sheep and cattle business had grown. There was even a sheep-shearing station next to the freight yards. A dozen or so new houses were built in a ring around the great grove of trees. His brother George, whom he hadn't seen for a number of years, greeted him. George and Mary lived in the big house George had built on the hill. With the direct rail connection to Chicago, cattle, sheep, and raw wool could be shipped directly to market, faster and cheaper.

William envied George and Mary, for they seemed to have such a happy home life. His own domestic life was cool and distant. William's visits to Monarch were always welcomed. He loved his niece and nephews, and they delighted in his coming. His favorite was his niece Amy. Together they took long walks, and talked of many things. It was always sad to leave, but there was railroad business to attend to.

On one trip, William attended the last-spike ceremony at Phosphate, Montana. The *Chicago, Madison, St. Paul & Pacific* was now a truly transcontinental railroad. He returned to Chicago well pleased with this final expansion.

William's dream had come true and, like all dreamers, he was forever dreaming bigger and better dreams. Now he would make his railroad the best, fastest and most efficient transcontinental railroad in the country.

AMY ASHMEAD

I sat in the sunshine, my back against the old stone wall, and looked over what had once been a beautiful garden. Along the valley I could see the old railway right-of-way. I could imagine cattle and sheep in the far fields. It was warm and very pleasant sitting there, and I dozed and dreamed—dreamed of sitting on the terrace drinking cool lemonade. I could hear voices behind me, voices from the past urging me to tell of another dream. The sun slipped behind a cloud, and a cool wind crossed my face, waking me up. I stretched and looked over at the valley. The fields were empty. Finally I stood and walked slowly down the road to my car. With the door open I sat behind the wheel, thinking, somewhat haunted by the voices. Whose dream would I tell?

I drove back to town, had supper and retired for the night. Later I awoke with a start to see a young lady standing by my bed. She was dressed in white. Her light-brown hair was fastened back by a large blue bow. The apparition seemed to say, "Remember those letters tied up with a blue ribbon? Read them again." I sat up, but she had vanished. I reached for my glasses and wrote down what I could remember.

• • •

Monarch was a lovely town, dominated by the great trees in center square and the mansion on the hill. The Ashmeads were large landowners and cattle ranchers. George Ashmead was founder and president of *The Ashmead Ranch and Cattle Company*. It was the largest and most profitable cattle and sheep ranch operation in the state. Twenty years before, brother William and a group of Chicago investors had extended the very profitable *St. Paul Railroad* west, through the rich ranch country of eastern Montana, connecting the Ashmead ranch and other ranches with eastern markets and the Pacific Coast. The area prospered and the Ashmeads became very wealthy. Small towns sprang up along the right-of-way, but none as pretty or as prosperous as Monarch.

Amy, the only daughter of George and Mary Ashmead, grew up in Monarch. At fifteen, she was medium height, with light-brown hair and blue eyes, like her father. She was a very beautiful young lady, an honor student in the senior class of the local school. Her two older brothers had finished school and now worked with their father on the ranch.

Amy stood on the balcony of the family house overlooking the valley. The river wound lazily toward the Musselshell, some miles distant. It was a lovely day. White puffy clouds floated in the sky, flowers bloomed in the garden and in the dooryards along the main street. Amy often stood on the balcony and dreamed. She loved the view and could see all manner of things: the sheep grazing in the field across the river and, if she walked to the end of the balcony, the cattle in the neighboring pasture.

Whenever Amy walked down to the station or the store, she paused at Jacob's church. She loved the little church and often went in. There was her grandfather's staff on the wall. She smiled as she sat in one of the pews, eyes closed, offering a silent prayer to St. Jude. She dreamed dreams of faraway places, of taking the train east or west. But she loved Monarch; it was home.

Every morning, when the school bell rang, she hurried down the hill to the school. The school was a two-storey brick building with a bell tower on the roof. There were two large trees, one on either side of the main door. Inside, it was cool and smelled of freshly waxed floors and furniture polish. Out back was a playground and ball field. The school was a pleasant place. Amy walked home for lunch, as did the other students. After lessons were finished in the afternoon, the boys played ball and some of the girls would wander down to the station. There was always an afternoon train, sometimes a freight with cattle cars to be switched onto the sidings, where cars loaded with sheep and cattle waited to be shipped to the eastern markets. Three times a week the mail train came steaming into town. Sacks of mail and packages were unloaded. The local postmaster piled them all on his cart and trundled them across the street to his post office and general store. Sometimes passengers got off, perhaps Uncle William on some railroad business, or a sheep buyer. If it was Uncle William, Amy rushed to greet him. Then they would walk home together.

The girls who had gathered on the platform one spring day watched all this activity. Amy slipped along the platform toward the engine. Sometimes Rob Ringling, a handsome young fireman, a few years older than Amy, would be on the train. He would climb down from the cab and together they would walk along the track talking of many things, or they'd slip behind the freight shed for a kiss or two. When the engineer blew the whistle they hurried back. Amy stood beside the tracks watching the train as it pulled out of the station. Rob leaned out the window for one last wave. He was wonderful, exciting, and Amy loved him dearly. To Rob, Amy was the most beautiful and interesting girl he had ever known.

Their walks together were always a joy. On Saturdays Rob would sometimes ride his bicycle to Monarch. Then he and Amy would wander down by the river, or have a picnic in the woods. Amy's mother was not at all pleased with Rob, for she felt that Amy was too young for flirtation of this kind.

When school was over for the year, the graduating class walked in solemn parade from the schoolhouse down to the town grove. The girls were dressed in new, white, starched dresses with large blue bows in their hair, and the boys in dark suits and white shirts with stiff collars and ties. They sat in two rows and listened to the speeches by the principal and the chairman of the board of trustees. Most of the girls in the class were getting married, and the boys would work for one of the local ranches or the railroad. Amy gave the valedictory speech. She looked out over the gathering and saw Rob standing in the back row. Her heart skipped a beat. After the speeches and the reception, Amy looked again for Rob, but he had disappeared.

All the family gathered for dinner that night. Uncle William had come from Chicago. There was much gaiety and laughter. After dinner her father and mother took Amy into the study. This was a cheerful room, which opened onto the garden. The scent of flowers filled the room. Uncle William was sitting by the open window smoking his evening cigar.

"Amy," her father began, "your mother and I feel that it is time you left Monarch and went to boarding school. You have finished your schooling here and there is no opportunity for further education. We want you to finish high school."

Amy was resigned to this, and there were good schools in Musselshell and Lewistown. Going to either place meant that she could come home for the weekend. Her father went on.

"We have decided to send you to Chicago to live with Uncle William and Aunt Victoria and attend Miss Dawes' *Finishing School for Young Ladies*. Uncle William is returning to Chicago tomorrow, and you are to go with him and make arrangements. Then you can return for the summer until the school session begins in September."

Amy's heart sank. She burst into tears and fled the room. Upstairs she flung herself down on her bed and wept bitterly. Leaving Monarch was bad enough, but a year without seeing Rob was more than she could bear. Her mother came into the room and sat on the bed.

"It is for your own good, dear. You're too young to get married and there are no nice boys here in Monarch."

"But mother," Amy choked out, "you married father when you were barely eighteen!"

"Yes dear, but that was different. Your father and I had known each other for a very long time, and he didn't propose to me until he had the ranch."

A train whistle sounded from the direction of the station. Amy buried her head in her pillow. Why was everyone so hateful? Her mother left the room quietly. Amy got up, washed her face and sat down at her desk and wrote. It was to be the first of many love letters to Rob.

The next morning the family wagon drew up to the front door. Amy's cases were loaded in the back. She and Uncle William climbed onto the seat and drove to the station without saying a word. Amy didn't look back for she could not bear the sight of her parents standing by the door waving. In her reticule was her precious letter. The driver piled the baggage on the platform, and Uncle William went inside to talk to the agent. Amy walked to the end of the platform. She waited as the engine pulled to a stop. Rob jumped down and ran over to Amy. She led him behind the freight house and handed him the letter.

"Hold me tight, and kiss me, Rob. I'll miss you, I love you!" was all she could say. They kissed passionately. "The letter will tell you all."

"Oh Amy! I'll miss you too, for you are my true love."

They kissed again. Rob put the letter in an inside shirt pocket as Amy ran down the platform with tears streaming from her eyes. Uncle William looked worried, but didn't say anything as she hurried past him and climbed into the passenger car. The whistle blew and the train pulled slowly out of Monarch. At the next station they stopped for a crew change, and as the train left the station, Amy saw Rob standing beside the tracks with her letter in his hand. The rest of the trip was a blur. Two days later they reached Chicago.

The next two weeks were so full and busy that nothing seemed real to Amy. Uncle William and Aunt Victoria were very kind, and did everything they could to help her adjust to city life. Uncle William was away during the day on business but always came home for dinner. Aunt Victoria was a disorganized, intellectual woman, interested only in clothes, fashion, and gossip. After dinner they all went into the parlor for their after-dinner coffee. Uncle William read the paper and smoked his cigar, Aunt Victoria tatted, and Amy read or played the piano.

Miss Dawes' *Finishing School for Young Ladies* was an old brownstone house on a side street. Scrubbed, white marble steps surmounted by two rampant lions led to the front door. Miss Dawes was a very stout, prim, maiden lady of medium height. Her eyes were set close together, and her mouth was small. She kept her lips pressed together as if to prevent any unwanted thought from escaping. Her dyed black hair was pulled up in a severe bun on the top of her head. She wore a stiff, whalebone collar and an unfashionable brown dress with high-button black shoes. Her pince-nez dangled from her neck on a black velvet ribbon. She informed Uncle William, in a booming voice, that she took only the daughters of society into her establishment. She peered at Amy, her pince-nez wobbling on her nose. How would this uncultured child of the West fit into her school? Amy was placed in a class with the other new girls, under the supervision of Miss Vines, a tall, thin spinster. Her wispy gray hair was always escaping its pins. Her face looked like a dried apple set on top of a post. She spoke in a high-pitched, squeaky voice. William took an instant dislike to both Miss Dawes and Miss Vines. Miss Dawes reciprocated in kind. He was not at all sure that enrolling Amy in this school was a good idea. The next time he was in Monarch, he would talk with George and Mary.

After dinner that night, Amy excused herself and went to her room. She wrote a long letter to Rob, letting her feelings flow. She disliked to both Miss Dawes and Miss Vines. She felt that they were snobbish and prejudiced. The next morning there was a letter from Rob at her breakfast place. Her love hadn't forgotten her. Amy quickly slipped the letter into her lap and covered it with her napkin, hoping that Uncle William hadn't noticed. Uncle William had noticed, but said nothing.

It was a hot, still, humid day in late June. Heat seemed to envelope the city. Amy had declined Aunt Victoria's invitation to go to an afternoon tea party, claiming a headache. She sat in the dark study dreaming of wide-open spaces and blue skies. She felt utterly miserable and lonely, and longed to go home. Uncle William came up the front steps whistling. He walked into the study and saw Amy sitting there looking gloomy.

"Well, gloomy Gus, what's the matter with you?"

Amy burst into tears. She was homesick. Uncle William took her in his arms and comforted her. He was very fond of Amy and hated to see her unhappy. "I've got good news. Do you want to hear it?"

Amy sniffled, blew her nose, and nodded.

"We're going to Monarch tomorrow. I have railroad business to tend to in Butte. So now you go clean up for dinner and get your bags packed, for we are leaving on the early train."

Amy's heart leaped! She was going home! She threw her arms around Uncle William's neck and kissed him, then ran upstairs. William watched her and smiled. He hummed a little tune, and settled into his easy chair to read the paper. Aunt Victoria came home—full of gossip. She was surprised to see William home so early, but she had learned never to question his actions. William told her that he and Amy were going to Monarch, and he would probably be away for two or three weeks. They were leaving by the early train in the morning. She smiled, and said sweetly, "That's nice, dear," and then went on discussing the afternoon tea party. Aunt Victoria said goodbye to Amy that night after dinner, as she wouldn't be getting up early to see them off in the morning.

Next morning after a hurried breakfast, bags were loaded in the carriage and they were driven to Union Station. Both Uncle William and Amy were in high spirits. Amy felt free again and told Uncle William of her fears and dread. The miles seemed to fly by and before they realized it they were in Minneapolis, where they stayed the night in the best hotel. The next day the train made excellent time crossing the Dakotas, and late that night they were in Miles City. The closer they got to Monarch the more excited Amy became. Tomorrow she would be home. There was a slight cloud on the horizon, but she didn't want to think about that, so great was her joy of being home again. Uncle William left the next day, but promised to stop on his way back.

Amy was home where the sky was blue and land stretched from horizon to horizon without end. Later that week, on the pretext of picking up the mail, Amy skipped down to the station to await the mail train. Surely Rob would be there. Amy was standing at the end of the platform as the train came in. Rob saw her and jumped down, and together they walked down the tracks, hand in hand. At first they felt a little shy, and didn't say much, but all at once their feelings bubbled out. They had really only begun when the engineer blew the whistle and they hurried back. As the train pulled out of the station Amy stood for a long time watching it disappear around the curve. She felt all warm inside. Rob was her true love.

The Fourth of July celebration was a special occasion in Monarch. Every house was decorated with banners, streamers and flags. Tables and stands were set up in the grove. There were speeches, songs, fireworks, and a huge picnic for the whole town. A spitted ox was roasted slowly over a firepit, sending off delicious smells. All the employees of *The Ashmead Ranch and Cattle Company* were there. Uncle William had come in on the evening train to join in the festivities. It was truly a town celebration where everyone in the community took part. Amy and her schoolmates put on a pageant depicting the history of Monarch. In the evening there was music by a local band and dancing in the square, which lasted well into the night. Rob had come, and he and Amy danced and danced. Later, Amy kissed Rob good night and skipped playfully up the road to her home.

In bed, she was too excited to sleep. Amy Ashmead was head-over-heels in love with Rob Ringling!

ROB RINGLING

I enjoyed a quiet supper and a restful night at the old Montana Hotel in Delphia, a hotel used by railway construction crews. Delphia had been a division point on the railway. In the morning, after a very good breakfast, I walked down the street to the old station. Although it had been converted to a seniors' center, it was still painted in the bright company colors. But instead of tracks out front, there were flowers. I went in and sat down at one of the tables. It wasn't long before a group gathered for coffee and gossip. I listened. The talk was nostalgic, as most of them had worked for the railroad at one time. When I asked if anyone had heard of a Rob Ringling, the response was immediate. The Ringlings had lived in a white, two-storey clapboard house off Main Street, just down the way. It had burned down a number of years back. The Ringlings were a well-respected family.

Old Frank Ringling was a construction foreman on the railway, and his wife, Frances, had for many years been a much-loved teacher in the Delphia school. They had three children—two girls and a boy. The elder Ringlings had continued to live in their house after their children married and moved away. One cold, windy, November day the house had caught fire and burned to the ground, and both the elder Ringlings died in the fire.

Their son, Rob, worked for the railroad after school, then full-time after he graduated. The coffee-table folks remembered him as a very likable young chap, and a strong union man. He had married the daughter of a cattle rancher down the line and they moved to Chicago. Their memories were vague about what happened after that. They knew his death was marked by something tragic, but they weren't quite sure what it was. I was grateful for their help and thanked them all before I left. Once outside, I found the side street off Main, and stood for a moment by the old foundation hole of the Ringling house. I had found my story.

• • •

Rob Ringling was the only son of Frank and Frances Ringling of Delphia. He was a quiet young man, of medium build, with sandy hair and brown eyes. He was not handsome, but had a pleasing manner. His parents demanded high standards. Their children had to do their best in everything they attempted. Rob, being the only son, felt that he never quite lived up to his parents' expectations, and that they were disappointed in him. He graduated from the Delphia high school with average grades, while both his sisters were straight-A students. After graduation he worked for the *St. Paul Railroad* as yard fireman. He worked hard, learned on the job, and was good at what he did. One day in May, the yard foreman told him to report to the east-end dispatcher. He was to fire the eastbound express freight.

Rob picked up his lunch bucket, which his mother had packed, and walked down the street to the station. This was his first day as firemen on one of the big mainline freight engines. Here was his chance to prove to his parents that he could handle the job.

The big black shiny engine, number 225, stood huffing and puffing on the tracks. As Rob climbed aboard he reached out and patted the red and gold company shield on the side of the cab, then stuffed his lunch bucket under the seat. The engineer climbed into the cab and scowled at Rob. A rookie fireman, that was all he needed this morning. This was an express freight run.

He looked at Rob and growled, "You ever fired before?"

"Only on smaller engines, sir."

"We have a long run and I'll need all the steam we can get."

"Yes sir. I'll try."

"Don't waste my time with silly questions, and don't make any mistakes."

Rob checked the firebox, the gauges, and all the valves to see if everything was in working order. The engineer sat by his window, saying nothing more, just watching. The signal light changed, the engineer blew the whistle and the great engine started to roll slowly down the track. Faster and faster it went, heading east. Rob was kept busy maintaining steam.

At the end of the run the engineer looked at him, nodded, and just before climbing down from the cab he growled, "You done good, young'un. You ride back with me tomorrow and we'll talk."

"Thank you, sir," was all Rob could say.

Thus began Rob's long career on the mainline of the *St. Paul Railroad*. He worked hard and was proficient at any job assigned to him. Usually, on the western run to Delphia, they dropped off empty cattle cars at Monarch. The loaded cattle cars were picked up the next day on the eastern run. One day a young girl was standing on the platform. Rob got down and smiled at her. She smiled back. He thought she was very beautiful and worth knowing, but he felt a little shy. As she always met the train, he discovered that her name was Amy.

Rob looked forward to seeing Amy when his train stopped in Monarch. Sometimes they walked down the track, or slipped behind the freight shed for a quick cuddle. They always seemed to have plenty to talk about. Rob loved Amy, and thought she was the most fascinating girl he had ever known. She gave meaning to his life. Those nagging doubts of inadequacy seemed to vanish when he was with her. The engineer smiled to himself and gave the two lovebirds as much time as he could before he blew the whistle.

Rob rode his bicycle to Monarch on Saturdays just to be with Amy. They walked beside the river, or in the woods, talking and holding hands. Sometimes Amy brought a picnic lunch, which they ate by the river or sitting among the trees.

When Amy graduated from school, Rob rode over from Delphia. He could stay for the graduation ceremony, but then had to hurry home. The day after graduation, Amy was at the station when the passenger train for Chicago pulled in. Her eyes were puffy and red from crying. Rob was concerned, but she pulled him behind the freight shed and told him that she was going to Chicago with her uncle, that she was going to school there. She gave him a letter and kissed him full on the lips. He held her very close, then watched as she ran down the platform and boarded the train. The tear-stained letter told him she was being sent to a finishing school in Chicago, and would be gone for a year. Rob put the letter in his shirt pocket and when he got home he wrote Amy a long letter, pouring out his love. Amy's reply soon came, telling of her dreadful experience at the Finishing School. Her descriptions of Miss Dawes and Miss Vines made Rob laugh. Many letters went back and forth. He treasured Amy's letters and kept them in his top bureau drawer, tied with a blue ribbon. They were from his true love, the light of his life.

Much to Rob's delight, Amy came back for the summer, and they met in Monarch for the July 4th celebration. After the barbecue and fireworks, the local band played dance music until midnight. He and Amy danced together all evening. After the dance he kissed her good night and took the midnight freight back to Delphia.

Rob hated to think about September, when Amy would leave for Chicago. It would be a long year. Rob had friends, acquaintances and fellow workers, but nobody filled him with love like Amy. He felt like he had lost his heart. With Amy gone, he threw himself into his work. He took and passed all the examinations that the railroad offered. He rose steadily through the ranks. He advanced from fireman to trainman, first on the freights, then on the passenger trains. Rob was well liked and respected by fellow workers. He was fair and honest in everything he did, and took an active role in the local union.

At one point, the local and the railroad had a very difficult and tricky problem to solve. After reaching an impasse they broke off negotiations. The president of the local, who was very fond of Rob, talked to him about the stalemate. Rob said he had a few ideas that might work. The president asked the railroad to reopen negotiations, and invited Rob to join them at the table. The discussion went back and forth, and finally both sides accepted Rob's suggestions. The union and the railroad reached a very fair agreement. All through the negotiations Rob tried his best to be fair to both sides. After that, most disputes were solved quickly and easily. However, at the end of every session, doubts of anxiety crept into his mind. Was he being fair? Was he being honest? Had he done his very best? Would his father be proud of him? But when he thought of Amy, all his doubts retreated.

Amy returned to Monarch at Christmas—to stay for good. For the next three years she attended the high school at Lewistown, graduating with honors. Upon graduation she went to work in the Monarch post office and store. She was always at the station when the Rob's train pulled in. How Rob loved to talk to her! And Amy listened with love in her heart. Rob wanted to marry her, but was he worthy of her love? Could he make her happy? The feelings of inadequacy were hard to overcome. However, when he was with his true love, all his fears and worries vanished.

MICHAEL O'CONNOR

IT was cold. The raw wind blew little dust devils down the street. I turned up my coat collar as I walked toward the great Union Station. The waiting room was full of ghosts, hovering near the high, vaulted ceiling. The room itself was empty except for a few straggling commuters, and the once-busy ticket windows were closed. I wandered around the deserted halls feeling there was a story here, but it was elusive. I took a dirty elevator to the eighth floor and walked down the hall to the old offices of the *St. Paul*. A lonely clerk sat behind a high desk listening to rock music on his boom box as he gazed out a dirty window. There was nothing much in the office. Gone were the paintings and the oriental rugs. Gone was the fancy furniture. I asked the clerk if I could see the historical archives of the railway. He nodded, reached across the desk, picked up a bunch of keys and led the way back down the hall. As he unlocked the door he said, "There. Help yourself. Let me know when you're finished and I'll come back and lock the door. Nobody will bother you. In fact, nobody has looked at these old records for years." With that he turned and walked back to the office.

The room was full of dusty old file cabinets, boxes, and other memorabilia. I began reading at random and soon uncovered a story of two men who tried their best to make the *Chicago,*

Madison, St. Paul & Pacific the best and most efficient railroad in the country.

• • •

Michael O'Connor was born on the south side of Chicago, of an immigrant Irish family. His father worked in the stockyards, and his mother took in washing. All too often his father would spend his paycheck in the local tappie, and come staggering home late at night. He was rarely abusive, just surly. Often there was little to eat, and certainly very little money. One day his father, still unsteady from the night before, fell into the stock pens and was trampled to death by the cattle. "Too bad," said the packing company.

Michael was forced to leave school and go to work to help feed the family. His education was minimal, but he had learned to read and write. He grew to be a handsome lad with flaming, unruly red hair. He had a charm about him that attracted people. His curiosity took him into new worlds and unexpected places. His education expanded. He read everything he could get his hands on. He would bring home books to read from the neighborhood library. Even at an early age he was known as a street-smart kid. He knew all the angles.

One day he found a job with the *St. Paul Railroad* as grease monkey and wiper. Every Friday he gave his mother his pay packet, keeping fifty cents for himself. Some of this he saved and the rest he spent on things he needed. He asked his mother why it was that some people were rich and others so poor. She had no real answer for him. They would talk long into the night, as she finished the day's washing and ironing. It was from her that he developed a social conscience. To her, all people were equal in the sight of

God. Class distinction, whether by money or education, was just not right. Michael always remembered this.

One hot, sticky afternoon Michael was in the freight yard sitting on a barrel, fanning himself with his cap. It had been a long, hard, difficult shift, and he was hot and tired. He paid no particular attention to what was going on around him, which was unusual for him. He didn't notice a tall well-dressed gentleman walking around the yard. The man stopped in front of Michael and asked him what he did. Michael, remembering his manners, jumped down from the barrel and said he was a wiper, but he was looking to advance. For some reason he felt free to talk this man, and told him some of his ideas about the working conditions in the yard. The man listened carefully, nodding occasionally, and finally said, "Young man, I like your ideas. Come to my office tomorrow morning early and we'll continue this conversation. Here is my card. Ask for Mr. William or they won't let you in."

When Michael got home he told his mother what had happened in the yard that day. She didn't know who Mr. William was, but thought he must be important to have an office in Union Station. That night Michael took a bath and washed his hair, even though it was only Monday. In the morning he dressed with particular care, putting on a clean shirt and tie. His mother had pressed his pants, and he shined his best shoes. He plastered his unruly red hair down the best he could and parted it neatly down the middle. Picking up his cap, he kissed his mother and walked down the street.

When he entered the concourse of the great station, he paused to look up at the vaulted ceiling on the main floor, then made his way to the bank of elevators in the hall. The elevator operators were all dressed in smart liveries. He got off at the eighth floor, walked down the hall and presented himself at the *St. Paul* office, as stated on the card. Michael spoke to the clerk at the desk, who ignored him. He tried a second time and very politely asked to see Mr. William. The clerk jumped up and shouted at him, ordering him out of the office. Michael stood his ground and refused to leave. The clerk glowered at him and disappeared into a back office. The office manager came dashing out in a temper and ordered Michael back to work. Yardhands had no right to come to the office. Again Michael said very politely that he was there to see Mr. William. The office manager became very red in the face and shouted at Michael. Did Michael know who Mr. William was? No. Did he know that nobody saw Mr. William without an appointment? No. All this shouting made no difference to Michael. He had been told to come to the office and ask for Mr. William.

By this time the manager was in a rage. He sent the desk clerk, who looked as if he had just eaten a basket of lemons, to Mr. William's office and check with the secretary. The secretary stormed into the office and glared at Michael, then asked him what right had he to presume to see Mr. William, and ordered Michael out of the office. Only important people saw Mr. William!

Nobody had noticed that Mr. William himself had come into the office and was standing very quietly by the outer door, listening to all that was going on. The desk clerk, the office manager and the secretary were all furious that Michael, a mere yardhand, had dared come into the office, and ask to see Mr. William.

For a third time he was ordered to leave, but Michael stood his ground and repeated that he had been told to come and see Mr. William. At this point William Ashmead stepped out of the shadows and, without a word, took Michael by the arm, led him into his office and closed the door. The furious trio looked at each other sheepishly, and went quickly and quietly back to work. Mr. William's wrath was legendary.

William took off his coat and hat and hung them up. Michael stood near the door twisting his cap in his hands. He felt a little embarrassed and out of place. Finally William turned and pointed to a chair, and Michael sat down. They talked for over an hour about the working conditions in the yards, and the condition of the railway. Michael had some suggestions for improvement. William had others. At last William stood up, walked around his desk, shook Michael's hand and thanked him for coming.

"Michael," he said, "you are to go back to work and keep your eyes and ears open. Take notes of everything you see. Then we'll get together again, but not here, for we wouldn't want to disturb those fellows again, would we. Goodbye."

The desk clerk pretended to be very busy, and did not even look up as Michael went out the door. As the door closed behind him, the clerk looked up and snarled.

It was many years before they met again in William's office. Often they met in the yard or the freight shed, or in the local tappie, and once William came to the O'Connor house for tea. This was a great honor. Michael's mother put on a clean dress and her best apron. She laid a clean tablecloth on the kitchen table, and served tea in her best china. Their conversations were seemingly casual. William talked about the railroad, the stockyards, and asked Mrs. O'Connor what she had to do make ends meet. He knew what he was doing. He was grooming Michael for better things.

Changes were made, and Michael was promoted. He became a favorite of everybody, from the yardmaster to the lowest wiper. He was a hard worker, and he believed in the railroad. Michael was always cheerful and had a good word for all the people he worked with.

Early in the spring William came into the yard and found Michael working in the car shops. It was lovely day. They walked outside and down the tracks. William turned to Michael and said, "I'm sending you on a trip. I want you to ride the freights from here to the West Coast, and then come back by passenger train. Talk to as many people as you can. Take lots of notes. Keep your eyes and ears open, particularly in the Western Division. If you are ever asked what you are doing, just give some bland answer, but never say you are inspecting for me. I don't want anyone to know that I sent you. You are to leave tomorrow. Here is your rail pass and expense money. I will see that your mother gets your pay packet every week. She will be taken care of while you are away. If you need more money, wire me. You will meet my brother George and his family at Monarch. Give him this letter, please. We'll discuss all your findings when you get back. Good Luck."

William handed Michael two envelopes. One was the letter for George and the other, expense money. Michael put the envelopes in his pocket and returned to the shop, a little bewildered. He went home early told his mother of his mission.

"Mother," he said, "Mr. William said he would see that you get my pay packet every week. He also said that if you needed anything, just let him know."

The next morning, after a hasty breakfast he kissed his mother goodbye, picked up his bag and caught the 6:02 a.m. freight to Madison and St. Paul.

Michael rode the cabooses, he rode the engines, and he talked to conductors, trainmen, and engineers. He wandered the tracks, the freight yards, and talked to switchmen and yard workers. On and on he rode, listening to complaints, grievances, and accomplishments, always taking notes of places and names.

One day he rode into Monarch. Michael picked up his bag and climbed down from the cab of the engine. From Forsyth he had ridden the engine talking with the young fireman Rob Ringling and the engineer. A beautiful young lady with light brown hair and blue eyes was standing on the platform waiting by the engine. Rob followed Michael down the ladder, and introduced Michael to Amy. For a moment Michael had nothing to say. He just stood there, cap in hand, bewitched by this beautiful girl. At last he managed to ask where he could find Mr. George Ashmead.

"That is my father," Amy said, "and he's down by the loading ramps." It was a small station and a smaller freight shed, both painted in the bright company colors. Michael walked down the platform toward the sheep pens. The train had unhooked the caboose, dropped off a couple of empty cattle cars and picked up two full ones. Michael, bag in hand, walked along the tracks looking at everything. A tall man, wearing a cowboy hat and boots, was supervising the loading of cattle and sheep. He looked vaguely familiar. Michael asked politely if the he knew where he could find Mr. George Ashmead.

"I am George Ashmead," came the reply.

"Then, sir, I have a letter for you," and Michael handed him William's letter.

George took the letter, opened it and read it. Then he turned to Michael. "Welcome to Monarch. You'll be our guest for dinner and the night."

The train whistled and slowly pulled out of the station, heading west. Amy, who had been talking to Rob, ran to join her father and Michael. Together the three walked up past the school to the house on the hill. Michael liked the look of Monarch. It seemed so peaceful, with flowers everywhere. George was asking about his brother, but Michael wasn't really listening. Everything was so new to him.

Michael was shown to a big room with adjoining bath. He bathed and dressed in his best went downstairs. George, Mary and Amy were gathered in the library awaiting dinner. George offered Michael a drink, which he refused. Michael had never seen a house like this and he was a little overwhelmed. There were just the four at dinner. Michael could remember nothing of the conversation, for he only had eyes for Amy. They retired to the parlor afterwards, where Amy played the piano and sang. Michael was thrilled. He excused himself early on the pretext that he should get to bed because he had to catch the early train.

In the early morning there was a discrete knock on his door, and Amy called out that if he hurried he could have breakfast with them before going to the station. Michael packed his bag and hurried downstairs to find George and Amy at the breakfast table. Mary was busy in the kitchen.

After breakfast Michael thanked Mary for her hospitality; then Michael, George and Amy walked down to the station. The westbound freight was just pulling in. Michael swung his bag onto the caboose platform, turned and said goodbye to George and Amy. George invited Michael to come back anytime, and Amy smiled. The engine gave a whistle and the train pulled out of the station. Michael sat at the conductor's table and took out his notebook. His mind was too full of wonderful thoughts, so he sat and daydreamed of Amy.

Later Michael wrote William several long letters outlining his findings. From Missoula he wired William saying he would be home in about a week. The passenger express pulled into Union Station in the late afternoon. Michael walked home. His Mother was very glad to see him, and handed him an envelope that had been delivered the day before. It was a letter from William telling him to come to the company's suite in the Plaza Hotel the next morning. William and Michael spent all day going over the report. At last William stood up and stretched. He called room service and ordered an excellent dinner. When they had finished eating William took out his cigar, and looked at Michael.

"This is an excellent report and I thank you. I would like to make you an assistant to the superintendent of the eastern division. You'll be my eyes and ears on that division and you will report directly to me, but this is just between us."

Michael couldn't believe his good fortune. He left the hotel in a daze, trying to fathom the trip, Amy, and now this. He went home and told his mother everything that had happened, and of his promotion. Michael was on his way.

Amy Ashmead – Part II

I walked the streets of Chicago, past rows of dingy, brownstone houses. I turned down a cross street: more dingy houses. Half way down the block I found the *Finishing School for Young Ladies*. It had seen better days. Its facade was dingy, the front steps needed scrubbing and the brass knocker needed polishing. I mounted the steps and entered the building.

Pretending to have a daughter, I asked for an interview with the headmistress. She was a tall, severe looking, humorless lady of indeterminate years. The sole object, she told me, was to mold young ladies to fit into Chicago's high society. A secondary object, of course, was to groom these young ladies so they could find very suitable husbands. I rose from the chair, thanked the headmistress, saying I would be in touch, and left. Outside, I stood on the sidewalk taking long deep breaths of fresh air. The atmosphere in the school was stifling of both mind and spirit. I walked slowly down the street shaking my head.

• • •

Summer passed all too quickly. Amy dreaded going back to Chicago and Miss Dawes' Finishing School. She hated that school and Miss Dawes, and Miss Vines, and all the silly girls who went there. But there was one saving grace: she would be living with Uncle William, whom she loved dearly. Aunt Victoria was a nonentity. Before leaving Monarch, Amy sat by her window, thinking and planning. She had made up her mind that she wasn't going to stay in Chicago and attend that hateful school any longer than she had to. She would be so rebellious and so wicked that everyone would hate her, and her parents would have to take her out.

Uncle William met her at Union Station and they drove home in his carriage. Aunt Victoria welcomed her sweetly, but otherwise said little. The next day Uncle William drove her to the school in his carriage. All the girls gathered in the assembly hall, where Miss Dawes, in a booming voice, welcomed them. She reminded them that they were young ladies of Chicago society, and that they were expected to behave as such. They were to arrive at school each morning wearing a clean, neatly-pressed school uniform, with clean hose and polished shoes, and a coat, hat and white gloves. When Miss Dawes dismissed the assembly, Amy went with the other new girls to Miss Vines' classroom. It was a cheerless, colorless, ugly room, with dingy gray walls and a stained brown linoleum floor, which suited Miss Vines' colorless personality.

Amy took a desk in the back row, as far from Miss Vines as she could get. As the girls stood at their desks, Miss Vines, in her high squeaky voice, informed them of the rules of conduct. She expected every one of them to behave like young ladies and with proper manners and decorum. They were to rise when they were called upon to recite. Amy stood by her desk thinking of ways she could disrupt the class. Miss Vines said that young ladies in her class were to wear their hair done up in a bun. The next day Amy came to school with her long hair flowing down her back. Miss Vines was irate and sent Amy to Miss Dawes, who peered at Amy through her wobbling pince-nez and demanded an explanation. Amy simply said that she preferred to wear her hair that way. This was just the beginning. Every edict that came from either Miss Dawes or Miss Vines, Amy misinterpreted or disobeyed. She defied Miss Vines. She wouldn't speak to Miss Dawes. She didn't do her schoolwork, and what she did was sloppy.

Letters of outrage were sent to Uncle William, demanding that he do something with his unruly ward. After a final barrage of letters, Uncle William took Amy into the study and they had a long, private talk. She told him how much she hated the school. She explained why she was so rebellious. She talked of her love for Rob, and Monarch, and the great open spaces of Montana. William was proud of his niece. He liked a woman with spirit. Amy had a mind of her own, and knew what she wanted. He, too, thoroughly disliked Miss Dawes, whom he considered a pompous ass. To him, Miss Vines was just plain stupid. He felt the school was snobbish beyond belief.

Just before Christmas vacation, a formal letter on official stationary was hand-delivered to Uncle William, dismissing Amy from the school for insubordination and behavior unbecoming a young lady. Left unstated was Miss Dawes' opinion that young girls from the wild west were just too uncultured for her school. Amy and Uncle William rejoiced and went out to dinner and a concert to celebrate. Aunt Victoria was appalled at such behavior. A young lady was to be dignified and polite. Uncle William wrote a long letter to George and Mary explaining the whole situation.

Oh what a joy to be home! It was a Christmas to remember. In January Amy went to the boarding High School in Lewistown. In three years she graduated with an honors diploma, and that summer she got a job as bookkeeper and assistant postmaster at the local store. She knew everybody in town and thoroughly enjoyed working in the store. She would meet the train and walk with Rob, who had risen through the ranks of the railroad and was now a conductor. He was also president of the local union. His patience and honesty had brought labor peace to the railroad's Rocky Mountain Division. Rob was both fair and honest in everything he did, and Amy loved him dearly.

One Saturday Rob presented himself at the Ashmead house dressed in his best Sunday suit, a white shirt and plain tie. Amy thought he was the most handsome man in the world. He had been asked by the national union to go to Chicago to be their chief contract negotiator. This was a real honor. He had come to ask for Amy's hand in marriage.

Amy was beside herself with joy. George was in favor, but Mary was a little reluctant. Although she did like Rob, she wasn't sure if this marriage was suitable. Rob had already found a nice house on the north side of Chicago, not too far from Uncle William on one side, and Michael and his mother on the other. This pleased Mary, for Uncle William would be near and would keep an eye on the newlyweds.

Two weeks later they were married in Jacob's church of Monarch. *The Grove*, Monarch's weekly newspaper, reported as follows:

...The bride looked beautiful, dressed in a white satin gown with a medium train and veil, and carrying a bouquet of pink and white roses. The groom in a black tuxedo made a sharp contrast. The bride's brothers and the groom's sisters attended the couple. The church was filled with the Ashmead and Ringling families and relatives. All attended the reception in the grove, which was open to the town...After the honeymoon the happy couple plans to reside in Chicago.

The next few years were very happy ones for Amy. She and Rob loved each other very much. They enjoyed each other's company, and Amy hated it when Rob had to spend long hours on contract negotiations. She made a great many friends. They had two boys, George and William. Every summer Amy took the boys and went to Monarch for a month, and then spent another month in Delphia with Rob's parents.

The year that George was six and William four, was a terrible year. In November, Rob received a telegram from his sister saying that their parents had died in a fire that destroyed their house. He rushed to Delphia, but there was nothing he could do. He was very depressed and upset when he came home. Amy did her best to cheer him up. She hated to see him like this. She felt that Rob would soon regain his old spirit, but he sank deeper and deeper into the pit of despair. He lost all hope. He wouldn't eat. He would barely talk, because he felt that this was *his* problem to work through. He didn't want to go out of the house, and he refused to see any of their friends. He would sit in an upstairs room, wrapped in an old shawl, and rock. Amy would hold him and love him. She tried to talk to him, but he didn't seem to hear. The boys didn't understand, for their father had always been so eager and willing to play with them, but now hardly recognized them. Christmas was coming and there was no joy in the house.

Michael and his mother invited them all for Christmas dinner. Rob refused to go, but Amy took the boys and went to the O'Connor's for dinner. Michael and his mother did their best to make it a festive occasion, but it was a somber affair because Amy was worried about Rob. Afterwards, Michael walked them home, and Amy went upstairs to see Rob. She found him stretched out on the floor, dead. He was clutching her love letters, tied in a blue ribbon, to his chest. She didn't know that he had kept them all these years. Amy was not sure if it was suicide or not, but it didn't matter. Rob was gone. Distraught, she ran downstairs and called Uncle William, then took the boys into the study and held them close. Uncle William and the funeral director came and took Rob's body away. Amy sent the boys to the kitchen for some supper and then to play cards with the cook.

When she went back upstairs her letters were lying on the floor where they had fallen. She picked them up and burst into tears.

"Oh, Rob," she wailed, "if only my love could have saved you!"

She heard a call from the hall downstairs. Drying her eyes and still holding her letters, she went out onto the landing. There was Michael, dear Michael, looking up at her. She dashed down the stairs and rushed into his arms.

"Oh, Michael, what am I going to do?" she sobbed. He held her very quietly and tenderly. Then he took her by the hand and led her into the study. They sat there in silence for a long time, each absorbed in their own thoughts. Amy thought, *I can't live here any longer, but how will I be able to raise the boys? I'll go home to Monarch. We'll be safe there.*

Michael thought about how vulnerable and tender Amy was. He kissed her and held her close, and before he left he promised to come back if she needed him. Amy was in a daze. She didn't know what to do. She called Uncle William again and told him that she was going home. Uncle William told her to pack their things and move in with them until after the funeral, and he would send his car around for them within the hour.

"Don't you worry, my dear, about the arrangements. I've taken care of all that. The funeral will be day after tomorrow, in the Episcopal Cathedral, for Rob had a great many friends."

"I know," Amy said in a very small voice.

For Amy the funeral was a blur. She was dimly aware of Michael sitting on one side of them and Uncle William and Aunt Victoria on the other. Aunt Victoria was suitably dressed in black. She hadn't really known Rob, but this was family, and one had to show one cared. The Episcopal Cathedral was full to overflowing. There were so many people, all of whom were devastated by Rob's death. He had been so popular and respected. There were representatives from all the other Chicago railroads, a large delegation from the union, and many of Rob's friends.

The funeral cortege moved slowly down the street from the cathedral to Union Station. Uncle William arranged for a special train to take Amy, the boys, and the casket back to Monarch. Amy watched as they loaded the casket onto the baggage car. The engineer and fireman stood by the baggage car door, caps in hand. The engineer stepped forward and managed to say, "We're so sorry, Ma'am. We'll miss him, for he was a good man. And, Ma'am, he was one of us. You are in our prayers, and may God bless you and the boys."

Amy was very touched. She took their hands, but could say nothing. The men turned away with tears in their eyes and walked back toward the engine.

Uncle William and Michael helped Amy and the boys to board the parlor car. They were going home to Monarch. Amy had no idea what the future held. She only knew she was going home. They buried Rob in the Ashmead plot in the walled graveyard next to Jacob's little white church.

ROB RINGLING – PART II

RRIVING in Chicago the night before, I had planned a day of research in the Chicago Public Library and at the Historical Society. It was routine, rather dull research. I wasn't at all sure what I was going to find. There were still a few loose ends to check. I had just finished breakfast when the bell captain came to my table with a telephone indicating that the call was for me.

I was very surprised, because no one knew I was in Chicago. The pleasant voice at the other end of the line said the call was from the headquarters of the UTB (*United Trainman's Brotherhood*). They had set up an appointment for me to see the union president that morning, if that was satisfactory. I said that I would be there at the appointed hour. I was quite unprepared, for I hadn't expected such a call. Why would the union seek me out? I gathered my notebooks and tape recorder, and went to union headquarters.

The receptionist said I was expected, and ushered me into the president's office. The president, a pleasant man, rose from behind his desk and welcomed me warmly. After I had introduced myself and explained my mission, the president said, "I've heard of your research into the demise of a great railroad, and the dreams of the people involved. I've asked you here today to tell you the tragic story of Rob Ringling, the best contract negotiator this union ever had."

• • •

Rob rose quickly through the ranks, from fireman to trainman to conductor. He was well liked by everyone, especially by those who worked with him. He was pleasant and very easy to get along with. His fellow workers elected him their local union representative. From a national perspective his local was one of the best run. There was rarely any dispute in the Rocky Mountain Division or on the lines west. Differences of opinion were usually resolved quickly, and to everyone's satisfaction. Rob's reputation spread throughout the union. In all his dealings with railroad management he was fair and honest. He always seemed to get the best possible deal for both sides. At the end of a negotiation, Rob would go home and worry that someone might have gotten hurt, or that someone else might have felt left at a disadvantage, or that an important point had been overlooked. But these thoughts and doubts he kept to himself.

The national vice-president of the UTB heard of Rob's reputation and came to Delphia. He sat in on the local's meetings, and at the table during negotiations. He toured the Rocky Mountain Division and talked to a great many workers. Everyone had a good word to say about Rob. Toward the end of his visit he asked Rob if he would like to come to Chicago—as chief negotiator for all the railroad's contracts. Rob had never dreamed of such a promotion, and he wondered if he could do a good job and live up to the union's expectations. The vice-president reassured him that he was the man they wanted. There had been little labor peace among the Chicago railroads, and the union was desperate to negotiate good contracts for their members.

Rob resigned from the *St. Paul* and moved to Chicago. He was sorry to leave his home in Delphia. His fellow workers were very sad to see him go. They held a farewell dinner to wish him the best of luck and much success. Rob was excited about the prospects and the move. He loved the give-and-take of negotiating, but his doubts lingered. Could he possibly live up to the union's expectations?

Rob dressed up in his best suit and went to Monarch. He called on the Ashmeads to ask for Amy's hand in marriage. Amy was overjoyed. Her father, George, was in favor, but Mary had some reservations. Amy was so young. What did she know about life, particularly married life? In the end, however, Mary agreed. She liked Rob. He seemed to be such a steady, honest, hard-working young man. Rob and Amy were married in Jacob's little white church in Monarch. Rob had found a lovely house on a quiet street on the north side of Chicago, not too far from Uncle William, which reassured Mary.

One of Rob's first negotiations in Chicago was with the *Chicago, Madison, St. Paul & Pacific,* the eastern division. Seated across the table from him was Michael O'Connor. They looked at each other and Michael broke into a broad smile.

"I rode in the engine with you from Forsyth to Monarch a number of years ago, remember?"

"Yes, and you asked a bunch of questions. I remember."

"Quite right. I think we'll get along just fine."

"So do I."

They stood up and shook hands across the table. Rob and Michael became the best of friends. There were never any union problems with the *St. Paul* as long as Rob and Michael handled the contract negotiations. They both understood the railroad, the workers, and each other. Uncle William was very pleased with this turn of events. He was in the middle of the plans to electrify the western division of the *St. Paul,* which was a radical new departure for a major railroad and took all his time and energy.

Amy and Rob were very happy. They enjoyed each other's company, and they enjoyed doing things together. On weekends the whole family would picnic in the park, or attend a *Cubs* game, or go sailing on the lake. They lived in a nice house, set back from the street, not far from Uncle William on one side and Michael and his mother on the other. They had two charming little boys, George and William. Every summer Amy took the boys and spent a month in Monarch with her family and a month in Delphia with Rob's parents. Life seemed to be very smooth and peaceful.

For Rob this was the happiest time of his life. He had a beautiful, loving wife and two charming children. He loved negotiating and was recognized by both union and management for his skill. Every major railroad asked that Rob handle their negotiations. All was going well, yet always in the back of his mind lurked the thought *What if I fail? What if I fail the union? What if I fail Amy and the boys?* The cloud of doubt and the fear of inadequacy were always on the horizon; he could never quite accept his good fortune.

One terrible day in November Rob's sister wired from Delphia that the Ringling house had burned to the ground, and that both his parents had been killed. Rob rushed to Delphia but there was nothing he could do. He became depressed and when he returned to Chicago he blamed himself for the fire, although he had nothing to do with it. The dark doubts were stronger now. Somehow he felt that he had failed his parents. He wasn't sure that he had ever lived up to their expectations. He felt hopeless and lost. The death of his parents made him feel unworthy and unloved, and because he had failed his parents he would surely fail Amy and the boys. At night, haunted by nightmares, he couldn't sleep. Amy would hold him, and reassure him. She hoped that together they could work through this depression. The black clouds never seemed to lift. The UTB granted Rob an extended sick leave but despair and depression crushed him.

Over the following weeks Rob sank deeper and deeper into blackness and hopelessness. He withdrew from active life. He became fearful and wouldn't leave the house or see any of his friends. He ate very little, and couldn't sleep. His appearance, always so neat, became slovenly. His whole being was haunted by guilt. Nothing had any meaning for him. Amy would hold him in her arms while he cried in desperation and despair. But did she love him, he wondered, or was she just being kind? He didn't know.

Amy, for her part, did her best to hold the family together, but it was very difficult. The boys didn't understand what was happening. Their father had become so distant he barely recognized them. How could Amy explain this to them? Amy herself was bewildered and frightened. She had no one to talk to. Rob was too far gone into his own black world of grief and guilt. Finally she turned to Michael and Uncle William for support and help. They both helped where they could.

Christmas was upon them, and there was no joy in the house. Michael and his mother invited Rob, Amy and the boys to Christmas dinner, but Rob refused to go. Wrapped in an old shawl, he sat in an upstairs room, rocking back and forth. When he wasn't rocking, he paced up and down the floor. After Amy and the boys went off to the O'Connor's for an excellent dinner, Rob roused himself with great effort. He could see no future. He was a failure. He stumbled over to the dresser. In the top drawer, under his shirts, were Amy's love letters, tied in blue ribbon. He had kept them all these years, and now he took them out and held them close to his chest. The letters from his true love—proof that she once loved him, but did she love him now? He didn't know. Nothing seemed real or had meaning, except Amy's letters. What good was he to anyone? He could see no way out. He was just a burden to Amy and the boys. In the medicine cabinet was a full bottle of sleeping pills. He poured them into his hand and swallowed them all, then carefully put the bottle back in the cabinet. Still clutching Amy's letters, he sat back in his chair. He became drowsy and he couldn't hold his eyes open or his head up. He fell over, out of his chair, and crashed to the floor. His tormented and tortured soul escaped his emaciated body, his hands still clutching Amy's letters.

After dinner Amy hurried home and rushed upstairs to find Rob dead on the floor. Amy wasn't sure whether it was suicide or not. He lay lifeless on the floor, holding the packet of her love letters tied with a blue ribbon. She hadn't known that Rob had kept her letters all these years. Was this his one piece of reality? Rob was dead. Amy was alone, with two boys to raise. She went downstairs and told the boys and held them close. She called Uncle William. He and the funeral director arrived and took Rob's body to the mortuary while Amy talked to the boys. She sent them to the kitchen for some supper, then she went back upstairs, and on the floor, where they had fallen, were all her love letters. She picked them up, sat in Rob's chair and wept. "Oh Rob, my love," she cried, "if only my love for you could have saved you."

There was call from downstairs. Amy dried her eyes and, still holding the letters, went out on the landing. Michael was standing in the hall looking up at her. Amy ran downstairs and threw herself into Michael's arms. "Oh Michael, Rob is dead, what am I going to do?"

Michael held her close until she stopped sobbing. Then he led her into the study and they sat in silence. Amy realized that she could no longer stay in Chicago, and she wanted to go home to Monarch. The house was too full of sadness and despair. She told Michael what she wanted to do and called Uncle William again.

She and the boys stayed with Uncle William and Aunt Victoria until the after funeral.

Rob Ringling had lived a brilliant but brief life. He was loved and respected by his family, his friends, and his co-workers. In the end, as Rob had become more and more depressed, life seemed to him to be utterly hopeless. The dark doubts of despair, guilt, and inadequacy finally overwhelmed him. He was buried in the Ashmead plot in the graveyard next Jacob's little white church in Monarch.

WILLIAM ASHMEAD – PART II

I came back to the *St. Paul Railroad* historical archives. It was slow going, but I turned up one piece of intriguing information. In front of me, spread out on the table were piles of dusty old papers that contained little new material. These were the records of the successful and profitable operations of the railroad—nothing extraordinary. However, tucked away in those papers I found a brief outline and a contract with the *Montana Power Company* to supply electricity to the *St. Paul* from Harlowton to Avery. I pulled a map from the shelf and studied it carefully. The Rocky Mountain Division of the railway was electrified over the continental divide and the Bitterroot Mountains. This was most unusual, for at the time, steam was king on all major transcontinental railroads.

• • •

It was a large office on the eighth floor of Chicago's Union Station. The windows on one side looked out over the main station tracks. From the windows on other side of the room you could see Lake Michigan. There were beautiful oriental rugs on the floor and striking paintings on the walls. On one side of the room stood a fine oak desk, decorated with a model of an engine. It was a fitting office for a railroad president.

William sat at his desk reviewing the cost sheets for the western division. The cost of coal had gone up and it was becoming expensive to keep helper steam engines on standby.

The continental divide and the Bitterroots presented real problems, for the grades were too steep for a single steam engine. What bothered him most was that he could see no immediate solution to this problem. There must be *some* way to reduce fuel costs. He rang the bell on his desk. When his secretary looked in at the door, William said, "Would you please ask Michael to come in."

Shortly there was a discrete knock on the door, and Michael entered. William waved him to a chair. "Michael, I want you to go on another trip for me. We have to do something about the expenses on the lines west. Coal is becoming too expensive. It's eating into our profits. I want you to go out there and see what you can find. Take up to a month, and we'll discuss the problem when come back."

"Do you have anything particular in mind?" Michael asked.

"No, I'm just baffled, and I know that something has to be done, so I'll be open to any suggestions."

Michael went back to his office, took a map out of the file, spread it out on the table and studied it very carefully. He left Chicago the next day. He rode all the *St. Paul* trains, passenger and freight. He studied the roadbed, the grade and the local economy. He talked with everyone who was connected with the railroad. After three weeks of trekking and traveling he stopped at Monarch. He hadn't seen George and Mary Ashmead for quite awhile, and he hadn't seen Amy since she moved back to Monarch after Rob's tragic death. He still remembered the day he had held her in his arms.

That night at dinner George mentioned that the *Montana Power Company* had just extended its electric power lines to Monarch. It suddenly became clear to Michael that here was the answer to the *St. Paul* problem. Why not electrify the railroad? That night he sat in his room with his notes and wrote a long report to William, giving his opinion and recommendations. The next morning, when he came down to breakfast, George and Mary had eaten and gone. Amy was sitting at the table. They talked until it was time for him to leave for the station, and walked down together. Just before boarding the train, he took Amy in his arms and kissed her.

As he rode back to Chicago, the report was temporarily forgotten. He was thinking only about Amy. She was so wonderful, and he was so in love with her. He promised himself that he would come back to see her.

William came in to the office early the next morning. Michael had telegraphed that he was on his way back and William was anxious to hear what Michael had to say. He paced up and down the office, fretting and fuming. Where was Michael? He called the reception desk, but was told that Michael had not come in yet. William paced some more. He sent a runner down to the station platform to check on the train. It had arrived on time, but nobody had seen Michael. Where was he? William was about to dispatch another messenger when Michael opened the door and came in. He had charts and maps under his arm, and a briefcase bulging with papers. All these he spread out on the table. William read the whole report without saying a word. Then he looked up. "Damn it, Michael, you've done it again. That's the answer. Now, let's do it. Let's electrify those lines west."

William was so excited he couldn't sit still. To electrify the lines was really a very radical idea. It had never been tried on such a large scale. There were trolley lines in the city, to be sure, but not on long-haul railroads. He got up, walked over to the window and stood looking down at the tracks. He smiled to himself, for the second half of his dream was coming true. The *St. Paul* would be an exceptional transcontinental railroad, with faster freights, better passenger trains, and bigger cargoes on its transcontinental service. He turned back to Michael. "I'm counting on you to supervise this operation, and to negotiate with the *Montana Power Company*. You know, together we'll make the *St. Paul* the best damned railroad in the country!"

Within a week Michael left for the west with a signed contract from the *Montana Power Company*. He set up his headquarters at Deer Lodge. Steam locomotives were very useful, and could haul heavy loads, but their daily range was limited to 100–150 miles and they had difficulty with power and braking in mountains. In extremely cold weather the engine's water lines tended to freeze, and they were susceptible to a number of other mechanical and servicing problems. Electric locomotives were far more reliable, and not limited by a fuel supply. This was the answer to the mountain crossings.

With electric locomotives, tonnage capacity doubled, operations increased, safety improved and maintenance expenses came down. From his office at Deer Lodge, Michael traveled up and down the division. He would occasionally slip off to Monarch and Amy, but every week Michael sent a progress letter to William. In one he wrote:

> *Electrification has been such a tremendous success that it's difficult to discus the results without seeming to exaggerate. Because of electric power, the St. Paul has forgotten that the continental divide exists.* *

There was a marked increase in both freight and passenger revenues. Passengers on the transcontinental could now ride in

An abandoned school at Vanada, MT.

A station with flowers instead of tracks, Alberton, MT.

An abandoned switch engine near Harlowton, MT.

An abandoned grain elevator at Delphin, MT.

An abandoned railroad right-of-way in Harlowton, MT,
looking west towards Two Dot, MT.

Abandoned freight yards, looking east, Harlowton , MT.

A roadhouse, now used for grain storage, Harlowton, MT.

A Little Joe locomotive near Deer Lodge, MT.

An abandoned freight station at Deer Lodge, MT.

Former Station, now used as a church, at Deer Lodge, MT.

smooth, clean comfort. Electrification was an accomplished fact. The results were more than satisfactory. William was very pleased.

One cool morning some months later, William came striding into his office. He was in a very good mood. He was still as tall and as handsome as ever. His hair had turned white, but it made him look very dignified and distinguished. He sat down at his magnificent oak desk. On his desk was a model of a bipolar electric engine, painted in the company's bright colors, a gift from Michael for his birthday. William had always admired it. The bipolars were the workhorses on the lines west.

William thought about his railroad, and realized that he had been president of the *St. Paul* for thirty-five years. He had seen his railway grow from a small mid-western granger line to a vibrant transcontinental line. He had instituted the use of block signals, and scheduled express freights from Chicago to the west coast. His rivals were left scrambling. Now it was time to turn over the reins of power to someone else, and the only logical person was Michael O'Connor. Michael had been executive vice-president for the last five years. Ever since that first meeting in the freight yard so long ago, William had kept a soft spot in his heart for Michael, who had finally begun to court his favorite niece, Amy, after she had been widowed by Rob Ringling's tragic death. He was still thinking about these things on his way home from the office.

William's wife, Victoria, was still beautiful, and she had become a gracious fashionable matriarch in Chicago society. After all these years she and William still had no common interests. She had her fashions and gossip; he, the railroad and the world. William had always dreamed of riding the *Golden Arrow* from London to Paris, the famous *Blue Train* from Paris to Istanbul, the *Crimean Express* from Savastopol to Moscow, and finally the *Trans-Siberian Railway* from Moscow to Vladivostok. Now the trip was becoming a reality. He had the tickets in his pocket—tickets that would take him around the world in the better part of a year. At dinner that night William told Victoria his plans. She said, as she often did, "Oh, that's nice, dear. Will you be gone long?"

Victoria had no conception of, or interest in, what these plans meant to William, and secretly she thought William a little dull, even a bit crazy. Why would anyone want to leave Chicago? Who would want to travel around the world by train—certainly nobody within her social circle! Her world revolved around fashionable Chicago society.

The next morning William walked into the outer office and stood by the door as he had so many years ago. He remembered the first time that Michael, a red-haired kid from the freight yards, had come to the office. He walked through to his own office. This was his last day. A month before, he had written and submitted his resignation to the Board of Directors. He picked up the phone and called Michael, asking him to drop by. Michael came in, still a very handsome man, his bright red hair now tinged with gray. William pointed to a chair.

"Sit down, Michael, and listen. I have resigned as of today and you have been appointed president. I leave you a railroad in good financial and operating condition. You know this railroad, and love it as I do. It is time for me to leave and it is up to you to carry on. I know you will be a great president. Now, Michael, here is my last presidential order: go home, kiss my favorite niece, give her my love, and tell her I'll come and visit when I get back. Then you are to take her out to dinner at our favorite restaurant. The reservations have been made and the dinner is on me. Here are tickets to tonight's performance of the Chicago Symphony. Enjoy!"

William got up, shook Michael's hand, put on his coat and picked up his hat and cane. At the door he turned and, after saluting Michael, walked out of the office. The next day he left for New York, and from there set sail for Europe.

MICHAEL O'CONNOR – PART II

I T was a lovely day in late fall. The sun shone warmly, and dry leaves were doing pirouettes down the street. I walked along the street looking at all the fashionable houses. This was the north side of Chicago, where the important executives and business leaders lived. I was looking for the house where Michael O'Connor, the last great president of the *St. Paul*, had lived. It was a beautiful, gracious house, set back a little from the street, surrounded by spacious lawns and majestic trees.

• • •

Michael stood in the hallway holding a sobbing Amy in his arms. He stroked her soft hair, and thought to himself, *This is my love. Ever since the day I saw her on the station platform at Monarch, I have loved her.* He held her very close.

"Oh, Michael, Rob is dead. What am I going to do?" Amy sobbed. He kissed her gently, wiped her eyes and led her into the study. They sat for a long time, each absorbed in their own thoughts. Michael knew that he would have to take care of Amy, but only when she was ready. Amy was thinking she couldn't stay in the house where Rob died and wondered how she was going to raise the boys.

She snuffled and wiped her tears. "Michael, I'm going home to Monarch. I can't live here anymore. After the funeral will you please sell the house for me? And see that our things are packed, and shipped?"

Michael nodded.

She looked up at Michael and said, "You *will* come visit me in Monarch, won't you?"

"Of course, my dear, whenever I can."

"Will you come tomorrow afternoon and help me take care of Rob's things, because I don't know what to do with them."

"I'll be here," he replied softly.

Michael's heart ached with love, but he did not dare move too quickly. He got up, kissed her, and together they walked to the front door.

"Call me anytime you want, and I'll come."

"Oh, Michael, thank you."

He hated to leave her alone, but he had to, for this was not the time to propose. He walked down the street to his own home, absorbed in thought. His heart ached, for Amy was so lonely and so vulnerable. He was glad she was going back to Monarch, although he'd miss her terribly. It would give her a chance recover from the shock of Rob's death.

Amy closed the door and leaned against it. Michael was there. He would help her. She called Uncle William and told him of her decision to go back to Monarch. Rob would be buried there.

Uncle William loved his niece very much, and she him. He always had kindly words of advice and comfort for her. "Pack your things, my dear, and I'll send the car around for you and the boys in an hour. You can stay with us as long as you want." Amy thanked her uncle and set down the phone. With Michael and Uncle William, she could make it through.

At the funeral, Michael sat beside Amy and the boys. He stood by her side as hundreds of people offered their sympathy and condolences. The funeral cortege transported the casket from the Episcopal Cathedral to Union Station, where Amy and Michael watched as the casket was placed inside the baggage car. The engineer and fireman stood nearby, caps in hand. The engineer stepped forward and offered his sympathy and condolences. Tears filled Michael's eyes as he escorted Amy and the boys to the private parlor car. He watched the train pull out, and his heart went with them. When would he see Amy again?

William and Michael were busy with the radical plans for electrification of the lines west. Michael spent the better part of a year on the road. He traveled all the lines of the *St. Paul* from Chicago to Seattle. He set up his office in a back room of the Deer Lodge freight station. From there he could supervise the progress of electrification. During these months he made a point of stopping at Monarch to see Amy whenever he could. His final report was at last finished. Electrification of the lines west was complete and operational. The brightly-colored Bipolars had no difficulty hauling trains over the mountains. He packed up, closed his office and headed back to Chicago, but he had one more stop to make.

There were very few passengers at the Monarch station, just a handful of cattle buyers waiting to board the train. He picked up his bag and walked past the grove, past the church and the graveyard, past the school and up to the big house on the hill. He had made up his mind to ask Amy to marry him, but would she accept him? He had carefully planned and rehearsed what he was going to say when he saw her. At his knock, Amy opened the front door.

There she stood, in cowboy boots, jeans, and a blue work shirt that revealed her lovely figure. She wore no makeup, and her light brown hair was tied back in a ponytail. To Michael, she was the most beautiful woman in the world. His mouth was open but he was speechless, and nervous, which was unusual for him. His fancy speech forgotten, he fumbled with his hat and dropped it. Then he stumbled over his suitcase. He had been a bachelor for so long that he didn't know quite what to do. He wanted to take Amy in his arms, but he suddenly felt very shy and insecure.

Finally Amy lead the way to the library, and Michael began to speak. But he could only stammer and blush. Amy smiled and took his hands. Looking up into his face she said, "Dear Michael, of course I will. Just ask."

"Oh Amy, will you marry me?" he blurted out, embarrassed to be so tongue-tied.

"Michael, my love. I have waited a long time for you to ask me. Of course I will. I would love to be your wife."

A great weight suddenly lifted from Michael's shoulders. He felt light-headed and giddy. He swooped Amy up in his arms, held her very close, and they waltzed around the room. Finally they both sank exhausted onto the chesterfield. Amy's mother, Mary, came in and wanted to know what all the noise was about. They both started to explain. Then Amy, beaming with joy, exclaimed, "Oh mother, Michael has asked me to marry him and I am so happy!"

Mary hugged her daughter, for she knew how very lonely Amy had been since Rob's death. Taking them both by the hands, she smiled and said, "I am so pleased. Just wait till we tell your father!"

At dinner that night Amy and Michael could barely contain their excitement and joy. And George was pleased, for he had always liked Michael. They discussed the wedding, whether it would be in Chicago or Monarch. All agreed that it would be held in Jacob's church. First, Michael had to go back to Chicago and submit his final report. George called William and told him the good news.

Three weeks later Michael and Uncle William arrived in Monarch. It was a beautiful wedding: a handsome groom, a radiant bride, and the whole town turned out to celebrate.

Their honeymoon over, the happy couple settled in Michael's house in Chicago. In due course Michael was appointed executive vice-president in charge of operations.

The *St. Paul* was running very smoothly and profitably. Electrification of the lines west had been a great success. They were able to cut the transcontinental running time, increase the freight tonnage, and provide transcontinental passenger service that was clean, efficient and comfortable. The *St. Paul* was the model of innovation for other railroads. Michael had come a long way from the tenement on the south side, and now he was happily married and doing work he loved. For William's birthday, Michael gave him a model bipolar electric engine, the one that was making the lines west famous.

Michael's office was painted in soft colors, with a subtle pastel rug on the floor. The windows looked out onto the streets of Chicago. He was sitting at his desk going over maintenance reports, when the phone rang. William wanted him to come by. Michael went down the hall to William's office and found him standing by the window looking down on the tracks. When William turned around he told Michael he had resigned.

Michael was speechless. William went on to say that Michael had been appointed president. Michael blinked. He couldn't believe what he was hearing. After William explained, he picked up his hat, coat and cane, shook Michael by the hand told him to go home and take Amy out to dinner and the symphony—all on William, of course. He moved to the door, saluted Michael and walked out.

Michael took a deep breath, and went back to his own office. He was now the president of the *Chicago, Madison, St. Paul & Pacific*

Railroad! He grabbed his hat and coat and left the office. Outside he hailed a cab and rode home in a daze. When Amy met him at the door, he swept her up in his arms and told her the good news.

Michael settled into the president's chair very easily. He followed the general practices that William had laid down, but with differences. The railroad had conducted an active and aggressive advertising campaign promoting the agricultural potential of the region they served. Over 7,000 new farms and ranches were established as people flooded in to settle the rich lands of eastern Montana.

When war was declared in 1917, the federal government commandeered all the country's railroads. These were difficult times for the *St. Paul*, for replacement parts and new rolling stock were almost impossible to procure. But in spite of this the railroad ran smoothly and efficiently. The sheep and cattle business was still as strong as ever. The *Ashmead Ranch and Cattle Company* was in full production.

William had returned from his round-the-world trip just before the United States declared war. Shortly afterwards, Aunt Victoria passed away from over indulgence, and was mourned by Chicago society. At the beginning of the new decade George Ashmead had also passed away, leaving the ranch to his boys. For a time, Mary came to live with Michael and Amy, but the call of Monarch, the wide-open spaces, and the endless sky were too great and she returned home. The same year saw the beginning of a three-year drought that crippled agriculture and ranching. A third of the earlier migrants left the dry plains to settle elsewhere. The *Ashmead Ranch and Cattle Company* survived, but only on a reduced scale. The *St. Paul* struggled with reduced revenues and soaring costs, and eventually Michael and the Board of Directors were forced to declare bankruptcy. Michael hated to do this, but it was the only way to restructure the debt. The railroad's creditors, now in control, asked Michael to stay on as president, thus assuring the railroad's smooth operation.

1929 was a disastrous year, not only for the United States, but for the world as well. The economy went into a deep depression that lasted ten years. The *St. Paul* continued to roll despite cutbacks of schedules, layoffs, reduced salaries, and the lack of new rolling stock. The railroad actually made slow gains to recovery. Michael insisted on track maintenance, for as he always said, *You can't run a railroad on poorly maintained track.* Toward the end of the decade the economic situation improved, and revenues increased.

Michael was getting old, and he was tired. He still presented a striking figure. His red hair, what was left of it, had turned white. His eyes were as bright as ever and his step was still firm. He had been president of the *St. Paul* for thirty years, and it was time for him to retire. He and Amy had always wanted to cruise the South Seas, stopping at all those exotic little islands with bewitching, enchanting names. But the Japanese attack on Pearl Harbor put an end to their dreams and plunged the country into another world war. Again the Federal Government commandeered the country's railroads, and Michael was asked to stay on as president of the railroad for the duration. He agreed with one condition, that his resignation would become effective the day the war was over.

The Japanese surrender was signed on the *USS Missouri* in Tokyo Bay on a September morning. That afternoon Michael surveyed his office, then put on his hat and coat. He picked up the model bipolar engine from his desk, handed his keys to his secretary and walked out of the company office, down the hall, down the elevator and out through the main door. He and Amy left for Monarch the very next day.

The *Chicago, Madison, St. Paul & Pacific* was a railroad with a dream. For seventy years it had been under the command of two most remarkable and competent presidents, men with a vision: William Ashmead and Michael O'Connor.

AMY ASHMEAD – PART III

I sat in the cellar of the *Forsyth Daily Herald* building. Spread out on the table before me were copies of *The Grove,* Monarch's weekly newspaper—a treasure trove of information. I read about the everyday social activities of Monarch. As I was leafing through the old pages, I came across an account of the wedding of Amy Ashmead Ringling and Michael O'Connor. There was a picture of Amy, Michael, and the two boys. They were standing in front of Jacob's church, smiling and looking very happy. I smiled to myself. So Amy's fortunes had begun to improve.

• • •

Amy was back in Monarch after the trauma of Rob's tragic death. At home, her soul had begun to heal. The boys had become honor students at the local school. Amy worked with her father and mother on the ranch. She rode out every morning with her father and the cowhands. Sometimes her mother rode with them. It was so different from Chicago. Amy would stop and listen to the wind in the great trees, or sit quietly in Jacob's church. When Michael had railroad business in the West, he would stop by for a visit. It was always a joy to see him.

One Saturday morning Amy was about to go to the stables, when there was a knock on the front door. This was unusual, for the door was always unlocked and people came in at will. She opened front door, and there was Michael. He seemed flustered, ill at ease and nervous. He shifted his feet. He took off his hat, dropped it, picked it up and just looked at Amy with his mouth open. His red hair, usually combed, was all tousled. He had come unannounced. Amy had no idea that he was even in the neighborhood. He seemed hesitant and shy. Amy smiled to herself and led the way to the library.

Michael stumbled over his suitcase as he came in. He stammered and blushed. This was so unlike him. He seemed totally tongue-tied. Amy realized that Michael was trying to propose, and the sweet man didn't know how.

She took him by the hands, looked into his eyes and said, "Oh, Michael, of course I will. Just ask."

"Amy, will you marry me?" he blurted out, blushing like an embarrassed schoolboy.

She laughed and threw her arms around him. "Of course, my love. I've waited a long time for you to ask me. I know you didn't ask me before because you didn't want to hurt me. Michael you are just the sweetest, gentlest man in the world, and I would love to be your wife."

Michael, whooping with joy, picked Amy up and they danced around the room. Amy's mother, Mary, hearing the noise, wanted to know what all the fuss was about. Amy could hardly contain herself, she was so happy. She rushed over to her Mother, her eyes sparkling. "Oh, Mother! Michael has asked me to marry him. Isn't that wonderful!"

The whole family rejoiced, and it was decided that they would be married in Jacob's church. First, Michael had to go back to

Chicago and present his final report. Amy hated to see him go, for now she wanted be with him all the time. Three weeks later Michael, Uncle William, and Michael's mother traveled to Monarch. That dear old lady looked very nervous, for she had never been outside of Chicago, and the wide-open spaces terrified her. Amy's mother took her in hand and soon made her feel right at home. Amy and Michael were married in a lovely simple ceremony in Jacob's little white church. One of the reports in *The Grove* was written as follows:

> ...*Our Amy wore a simple, pale blue dress with matching shoes and accessories. She wore no veil and carried a bouquet of white roses. She was attended by her two sons. Her father, George, gave the bride away, and her Uncle William stood with the groom. The two mothers sat together in the front pew, teary-eyed. The church was filled with the people of Monarch. Everyone was invited to the bountiful reception in the big house on the hill. There was much rejoicing, for our Amy was getting married again.... After a short honeymoon the happy couple will live in Chicago.*

After the ceremony Michael, Amy and the boys walked into the walled graveyard and laid one white rose on Rob's grave. After their honeymoon they moved into Michael's house in Chicago. Michael had fixed up a nice apartment in the carriage house for his mother. Soon Michael was promoted to Vice-President in Charge of Operations of the *St. Paul*, and during the next five years Amy renewed her old friendships.

One afternoon, much to Amy's surprise, Michael came home early. He seemed dazed and bewildered. Uncle William had sent his love and said that he would see them when he got back from his rail trip. Amy wanted to know where he was going. Michael didn't know, but he did say that Uncle William had resigned from the railroad that morning, and that he, Michael, had been appointed president of the *Chicago, Madison, St. Paul & Pacific Railroad*. Then *Amy* was overwhelmed—and overjoyed. Michael had worked so hard for the railroad, and now he was being rewarded. But where was Uncle William going? Amy had to find out. She called his house, but he wasn't there, and Aunt Victoria had no idea where he was. She mentioned that he was following some crazy notion, but she didn't know what it was. She didn't even know how long he would be away.

When the war began in Europe, shortages began to affect their lives, first appliances and then food. The *St. Paul* was extremely busy, and Michael worked long hours. Shortly after the United States declared war, Uncle William returned home. He had been around the world, traveling on all the famous trains of Europe, ending with a trip across Russia on the *Trans-Siberian Express*. Aunt Victoria thought he was quite mad.

A few years later Aunt Victoria died. Amy was very sorry. She hadn't really known her aunt. There wasn't much to know except that Victoria was prominent in Chicago's high society. She and Amy had moved in totally different circles, and Aunt Victoria had never forgiven her "insubordination" at Miss Dawes' school. It was just unladylike!

After Victoria's death, Uncle William bought a small house on Lake Geneva and retired there, spending his days reading, writing and fishing. Amy and the boys would visit him over weekends or in the summer. She loved to hear him tell tales of his adventures.

The cattle business had boomed during the war. Amy's father, George, had been very busy. Now that the war was over he could take a little time off and rest. He had always worked hard, and he was tired. Her mother called one morning to tell Amy that her father had died. This was a great blow, for she dearly loved her father. The whole family gathered in Monarch for the funeral. Many of the townspeople spoke of George's generosity and kindness. He was much loved by those who knew him and highly respected by his many acquaintances.

Amy, her brothers, Michael, Mary, and the boys stood by the grave as George's casket was lowered into the ground, his on one side of the center stone and Rob's on the other. Mary came to live with Amy and Michael, but she missed the wide-open spaces and blue sky, and soon returned to Monarch.

Amy and Michael's boys, George and William, finished college and went on to high-paying jobs. George was a lawyer and William went into finance. Both prospered. During that period the *St. Paul* fared poorly. There was a drought in the west, and the farm and cattle business fell off. The railroad had to cut back on some of its services, and it took three years for revenues to pick up again. Then the United States and the world were plunged into a terrible economic depression. The railroad continued to operate, even turning a small profit, thanks to Michael's careful management.

After serving as president of the railroad for thirty years, Michael was ready to retire. He and Amy had planned a trip to the South Seas, a second honeymoon, but suddenly the world was at war again. The Japanese attacked Pearl Harbor, and the United States found itself at war with both Germany and Japan. The Federal Government again commandeered all the nation's railroads, asking Michael to continue as president for the duration. After talking it over with Amy, he agreed to continue, with the proviso that he would resign and leave on the day the war was over. For six long years the war dragged on. Then one clear

September morning, the final surrender was signed aboard the *USS Missouri* in Tokyo Bay.

Michael came home early that afternoon. He had resigned. Amy packed their bags, and the next day they left for Monarch. They were going home.

GEORGE AND MARY ASHMEAD

I walked along the dusty road that circled the great grove of trees, past old cellar holes, where flowers still bloomed and danced in the sunshine. I walked on to the little walled graveyard, climbed over the gate and walked among the graves, pausing to read an inscription here and there. I walked on until I came to a larger plot with a central carved stone. It had a single name carved into the base:

ASHMEAD

Around it were smaller stones of individuals. Here were George and his wife Mary Ashmead. Amy Ashmead with her two husbands, Rob Ringling and Michael O'Connor. Near the far wall were two graves, lying head to head. The modest headstone between them was carved with entwining vines and leaves. The inscription read *In the loving memory of Jacob August and Catharine Schultz Armour. May they rest in Peace.* Old Jacob had brought his beloved to Monarch after all. I sat with my back against the center stone and looked out over the town. It was such a peaceful place. Of the town of Monarch there was nothing more. All the people had moved away, the flowers grew wild, and all was quiet.

• • •

Monarch was in the center of the rich cattle country of eastern Montana. *The Ashmead Ranch and Cattle Company* had prospered. All of George and Mary Ashmead's dreams had come true, including Monarch, a beautiful town, just the way they had planned it. Those who lived here took pride in its beauty. George and Mary had built their big house on a rise of land behind the town.

They were still a handsome couple, and very much in love. Almost every evening they stood on the terrace holding hands, looking out over the beautiful garden and the valley. Every morning George would ride out with the cowhands, checking on the herds. Very often Mary would ride with him. She was just as good on a horse and with a rope as he was. This was particularly true on roundup day, when every hand was needed. They would all come home for lunch at noon and, in the summer, they would often eat out on the terrace. In the afternoon, while Mary tended to the household chores, George would go to the freight yards to supervise the loading of cattle and sheep for *Armour and Company* and other packinghouses in Chicago. Brother William's railroad had made all the difference.

The Ashmeads had two boys, and a few years later, Amy was born. All the children were excellent horsemen by the time they were ten—even Amy. She, too, loved to ride over the fields with her father and mother. Amy also loved Monarch and the great open spaces of the west. However, Mary was concerned that Amy was not getting the proper training a young lady should have. She wanted her daughter to be exposed to Chicago society and to meet some eligible men. Monarch, she felt, was too limited. She and George had discussed this many an evening as they sat by the fire. The question was—what course of action should they take?

In the spring Amy graduated from Monarch School. George was not sure about sending her to Chicago. There were two good boarding high schools close to home, one in Musselshell and the other in Lewistown. Why wouldn't they do? But Mary wanted her daughter to have all the advantages that a big city could offer. Amy could live with Uncle William and Aunt Victoria, although Mary didn't like Victoria. When Mary was growing up in Chicago, she felt that Victoria was a spoiled brat. On the other hand, Victoria *was* influential in Chicago society.

Amy had been seeing great deal of a young fireman named Rob Ringling. He wasn't the type of person that Mary wanted Amy to marry, and besides she was much too young to have a steady boyfriend. Rob came from a nice family, but not their class. George smiled at Mary. He loved her very much, but he didn't share her ideas on class and society. At last they agreed to send Amy to Miss Dawes' *Finishing School for Young Ladies* in Chicago. After graduating from Monarch School she would go with Uncle William to Chicago. When they told Amy, she reacted with rage, grief and a flood of tears.

Miss Dawes' *Finishing School for Young Ladies* was a disaster, as George thought it might be. Amy hated the school and the teachers. She hated Aunt Victoria, she wouldn't eat, and she lost weight. She was in a constant state of rebellion. Aunt Victoria didn't understand Amy. This was not the way a refined young lady behaved. Uncle William was worried, and expressed his concern to his brother George. He didn't like Miss Dawes' school or the teachers either. He thought they were a stuffy, snobbish, pompous lot. Amy came home for Christmas after having been formally dismissed from the school. This was a great disappointment to Mary, for she had visions of Amy shining in Chicago society.

In January, Amy went to the high school in Lewistown. She finished in three years and graduated with honors. In the meantime Rob had risen through the ranks of the railroad and the union. He was now the chief contract negotiator for the western division. Ever since Amy's return they had been seeing each other regularly. Mary tolerated this, but George was pleased.

Rob had been outstanding in his contract negotiations and had been asked to come to Chicago as head of the union's railway negotiations unit. One weekend, before he left for Chicago, Rob came to Monarch dressed in his best Sunday suit. He asked George and Mary's permission to marry Amy. Mary was very reluctant and was still not sure that this was a suitable marriage, but Amy was ecstatic. Rob went to Chicago and found a lovely house on the north side, not far from William's home.

Several weeks later Rob returned to Monarch. He and Amy were married in Jacob's little white church, and after the wedding they moved to Chicago. The Ashmead house seemed empty without Amy's cheerful presence. George and Mary's sons had married and were living in Monarch. Mary found great joy in her grandchildren. When she went downtown for the mail she would drop in on one family or the other for a visit. Soon Rob and Amy had two boys, George and William. Each summer, Amy would bring the boys for a month in Monarch and a month with the Ringlings in Delphia.

One November came the terrible news that Rob's parents had died in a fire that destroyed their home. Rob did not recover from this tragedy. Amy did her best under these very difficult circumstances, but she couldn't save Rob. He died on Christmas Day. Amy sold the house in Chicago and she and the boys moved back home to Monarch.

Michael O'Connor visited Monarch whenever he had railroad business in the West. During Rob's illness Michael had provided

Amy with the support she needed. After Amy moved back to Monarch, Michael made a point of visiting her whenever he was in Montana. He had loved Amy from the day they first met. On one visit Michael and Amy were in the library making such a noise that Mary came in and found them dancing around the room. Amy rushed up and threw her arms around her mother, blurting out that Michael had asked her to marry him. Mary was very happy for them, for she knew that Amy had been suffering from loneliness. George had always admired Michael and was very pleased. Amy and Michael were also married in Jacob's little white church. After the wedding they moved back to Chicago.

The ranch grew ever more prosperous. More cattle, sheep and wool were shipped from Monarch than any other place in the state. George and Mary were semi-retired, and had turned the daily operations of the ranch over to their sons. Brother William had retired as president of the railroad, and Michael had been appointed president.

When the United States was plunged into war, the demand for cattle and sheep increased. George had to go back to work, as many of the ranchhands had been drafted. By the end of the war George was tired. He and Mary had a beautiful, bountiful life; they loved and depended on one another. George counted on Mary for her wisdom and support. They had been blessed with wonderful children and grandchildren. Now it was time to rest. The boys could run the ranch.

George rode out one morning to follow the trails around the ranch. He and Mary had a favorite, secret spot at the edge of the woods overlooking the countryside. Here they would sit and dream. George had built a bench and carved their initials on the back. Sometimes they brought a picnic lunch, just to be together. On that morning George let his horse take him to this spot. He dismounted and sat on the bench under the tree, half dozing and remembering the early days: how the young Crow Indian warrior had led him to the site for Monarch; when he and Mary had lovingly planned the town; and how old Jacob had marked out the site for the church with his staff. He dreamed and slept.

When George's horse came home without him, Mary was alarmed. She saddled up her own horse and rode to the spot where she knew George would be. He seemed to be asleep, but he had quietly slipped away to that other world of peace. Mary sat holding him and wept. She stayed there a long time. Her George, the light of her life, her true love, had gone. They had been married almost fifty years—fifty joyous, wonderful years.

She rode slowly, sadly back to the house. She didn't bother to wipe away the tears that ran down her face. The day was not as bright as it had been. Her George was gone. She sent the boys with the wagon to bring their father's body home. The great double bed now seemed so empty. She listened in vain for George's footstep and his cheery voice.

The whole town came to the funeral. This was family. There were many testimonials to George's generosity and kindness. George was buried in the walled graveyard beside Jacob's little white church.

When the weather was nice Mary saddled her horse and rode out to their secret place. She sat on the bench overlooking the valley, and talked with George.

The Chicago, Madison,
St. Paul & Pacific – Part II

I had found the skeleton and the bones. I had heard ghosts whisper in the wind. I had glimpsed the soul of a great railway by listening to those who knew her intimately. I had shared their heartbreak as the tracks had literally been torn from their towns and communities. Ten years from now the story of the railroad will be only a memory. Bikers and hikers will wander over the old roadbed marveling at the engineering of tunnels and trestles, totally unaware of the soul of the great railroad and the dream that it represented.

•••

Once there was a beautiful young lady of modest means who was courted by many. She extended her charms to hard-working, industrious people, and was paid handsomely in return. Her appearance was always sparkling and bright. Those who knew her, loved her. She grew and matured, never venturing too far afield. She was ever gracious with her bounty, and all those who worked with her prospered.

A dreamer came by. He fell in love with the gracious lady and she with him. They dreamed together, and together they extended their horizons to the western sea. He flattered her and gave her many pretty and beautiful things. She responded to this generosity and together they grew rich and prosperous. Electricity was added to her domain, and her sparkle and brilliance became well known. There was happiness and joy in the domains of the gracious lady.

Her much-loved dreamer-companion died, but another dreamer was there to take his place. She fell in love with the second dreamer as she had with the first, and he with her. He knew this gracious lady well, as he had worked many years for her, tending her house and grounds. He gave her anything she wanted. The lady was brilliant and bountiful. They hit a rough patch when ready cash was scarce. The lady could no longer afford all the luxuries she wanted, but the everyday useful things were still there. She didn't mind for she knew that her lover still worked hard on her behalf. They slowly recovered from the rough times, and again this gracious lady, now older and wiser, responded with the same flair as before. At the height of her brilliance, her second dreamer-lover died. It had been seventy years that the lady had been cosseted, flattered and pampered by two men with vision and a dream. Seventy wonderful, bountiful years!

A third companion appeared. A bit of a dreamer, yes, but he didn't have the grand vision of the other two. He didn't give her the pretty things she wanted because he saw no use in them. He gave her only utilitarian things. This was hardly romantic, but the old sparkle was restored. Money was spent fixing up the house and grounds, polishing equipment. The gracious lady was still as beautiful as ever, but there were signs of age around the edges. Unfortunately, her latest companion left her for another lady of greater wealth.

Our lovely lady had two neighbors who lived on either side of her. They had attempted to keep up with her splendor and sparkle, and outdistance her bounty. They were not very successful in this competition; in fact they were rather dull. These two neighbors married in a lavish ceremony and combined their assets and domains. The two neighbors were greedy and wanted more. A new companion-manager by the name of "Heep" arrived to manage the grand old lady's affairs. He had worked loyally for one of the neighbors for many years. He was a smooth, genial character with excellent manners, but he was devious. He soon gained complete control of all the old lady's finances and assets. He would tell her that repairs to her house and grounds were done, when they were not. He would talk of new equipment purchased, when it was not. The useful things around the house and grounds began to wear out and were not replaced. Her manager came to her, complaining bitterly that the costs of running the estate were far exceeding the revenue. She must cut back on expenses and forego new purchases, even forego the replacement of worn-out equipment. The old lady didn't like this, but there seemed to be no way out. The electricity bill and other bills went unpaid, and the creditors complained. The hired help was laid off. Maintenance was deferred. She was told that the western part of her domain was too expensive to operate. The manager claimed it had to be abandoned, so they could improve the rest of the grounds.

One day her manager, all beams and smiles, came in and showed our gracious lady a check he had gotten from the sale of her western dream. It had been sold for scrap. The old lady cried. Her beautiful western dream was no more. It had been torn up, thrown away, and sold to small, greedy, grubby buyers. Buildings and stations were boarded up or torn down, and only a few old friends remained standing, neglected and forgotten. The lady took to her bed, feeling violated. Her heart was broken. No one loved her any more. She didn't know that her manager had been unfaithful to her, that he was a liar and a cheat, and that he had systematically stolen her property. She died destitute and forlorn. Those who loved her wept bitter tears and mourned her passing, for they knew what had happened. The dream was gone, stolen by small-minded men.

Now the dream lived only in the memories of those who had worked for and loved this gracious lady. Her traitor-manager presided over her passing. When it was done he smiled to himself, went to the phone, called the neighbors, and together they rejoiced. The death and destruction of the old lady's estate, which they had engineered, was now complete. The grand old lady was no longer a threat. Shortly after her death, her house was demolished and her property sold.

• • •

After Michael O'Connor retired, leaving behind a prosperous and profitable railroad, the Board of Directors appointed a series of mediocre presidents. Most of them had no dreams and little vision. For the next fifteen years the railroad recovered from wartime shortages and regained some of its past glory. The famous transcontinental passenger service was restored, with new equipment. New, more powerful electric engines (*The Little Joes*) were put into service. All seemed rosy. Montana had recovered from the depression and the war years, and the economy was booming again.

In the late sixties, the Board of Directors appointed a new president. He had been the vice-president of one of the rival railroads, and had been forced out when they merged. He wasn't interested in railroads, particularly the *St. Paul,* for there was no money in them. The merger of the two rivals spelt the end of the

St. Paul's lines west. Why have three competing transcontinental lines? Malls, property, land—that's where the money was. His policy was to close down the railroad, abandon all the western lines, sell the rest of the railroad at fire-sale prices and invest the money in land.

So it began. Maintenance on the right-of-way was deferred, engines and rolling stock were not serviced properly. Freight tonnage was shifted to other railroads, either by accident or design. The pride of the *St. Paul*—the transcontinental passenger service—was discontinued. There was a slow and steady decline in revenues. Management insisted it was the economic conditions of the times that prompted the cutbacks. Costs were higher than revenues, they said. The employees knew better. The two parallel rail lines competed with the *St. Paul* for transcontinental tonnage. Four years later the *St. Paul* discontinued the electric lines and switched to diesel, just as the price of diesel fuel doubled. This was a foolish, expensive move.

The *St. Paul* declared bankruptcy and abandoned all lines west of the Missouri. The company still had valuable assets but they were hidden from public view. The wrecking crews began in Seattle and came east, ripping up the track and tearing down power lines. Track, overhead wire, and rolling stock were sold for scrap. Stations were boarded up or bulldozed, and rolling stock was often abandoned on sidings. There was nothing left but ghosts. The *Chicago, Madison, St. Paul & Pacific Railroad* was no more.

Once there was a railroad.
They made it run,
Made it race against time,
Now it's done.
Brother, can you spare a dime?

MONARCH

O N my last visit to Monarch I walked around the old townsite, up past the abandoned schoolhouse to the ruins beyond. I stood looking over the valley and the river. Monarch, the beautiful, was no more. With sadness in my heart I walked back to my car, parked in the grove of cottonwoods.

• • •

George Ashmead died. His sons and grandsons then operated the still-profitable *Ashmead Ranch and Cattle Company*. Following World War I, eastern Montana suffered a three-year drought, which affected the cattle business. Herds had to be cut. Families left Monarch for better-paying jobs in the cities. Just as Monarch was recovering, the country went into a financial and social depression. Cattle sales remained depressed as eastern markets dried up. There was plenty of food and dairy products in Monarch. Most families had their own gardens, but there was a shortage of hard cash. The local store resorted to trade by barter.

The situation changed again with coming of World War II. Many of the young men of the town were drafted. The demand for cattle and sheep increased. There was money to be made and spent. The post-war prospects for Monarch and the cattle industry looked bright. After two of the Ashmead grandsons were killed in the Pacific, the family gave up the daily operations of the company and eventually sold it to a larger more affluent cattle company.

Upon Michael's retirement from the railroad, he and Amy moved back to Monarch. When they died, the big house was left empty. Their two boys, George and William, and their families, used it as a summer home.

The school closed for lack of students. Families drifted away to the cities. Monarch was still a regular stop for the transcontinental passenger train, but few got off and fewer got on. Cattle and sheep were shipped weekly to Chicago and further east.

First the passenger trains were discontinued, as few people rode the train anymore. Freight service was cut, from daily trains to a train every other day. The station and the freight shed needed painting; the roofs leaked. But no repairs were made. Track maintenance was deferred. The lines were embargoed, and in some places trains could travel at only 10 miles per hour. Then one day the trains stopped altogether. The big house was empty. Summer visitors had returned to their winter homes. The day after the last freight train went east, the big house mysteriously caught fire and burned to the ground.

Salvage crews came through, ruthlessly tearing up the track. A bulldozer demolished the station. The heart and soul of Monarch were gone. The remaining families moved away, and their houses fell into disrepair and ruin.

All that remained were the great trees, the flowers, and the graveyard behind its sturdy wall. Jacob's church had collapsed during the winter.

I stood among the ruins idly poking at debris with my foot. My shoe struck something hard and I bent down and dug around, finding the end of what looked like a branch. I pulled it out, wiped it clean and looked at it. It was the beautifully carved staff with a simple design of vines and leaves that I had seen hanging in the church. At one end were the initials *J.A.A.* and the date, and at the other end the initials *C.S.A.* This was Jacob's staff. I held it for a long time, thinking and dreaming.

The beautiful town of Monarch was but a memory. Flowers still bloomed every year in the forgotten dooryards, marking the site of what had been. I picked a bouquet of the prettiest and laid a flower on each of the six graves, two on old Jacob's and Catharine's grave.

I turned and stood, staff in hand, and watched the wild turkeys and rabbits; listened to the foxes barking in the fields. Nature had reclaimed the land.

I had slept many a night under the great trees. The little stone fireplace I had built on my first visit would be the only sign of my sojourn in Monarch. I packed my car for the last time, put Jacob's staff on the front seat beside me, and drove slowly around the road that circled the trees. I paused at the graveyard and said goodbye. It was like leaving old friends. I had spent many a day poking around the ruins, listening to the wind and reconstructing, in my mind, life as it had been.

Now I was leaving. When I came to the old right-of-way I stopped and listened, took one last look back, and wiped my eyes. Then I crossed the abandoned roadbed and drove out of the town.

Monarch, the beautiful,
Lay sleeping in the sun.
Once there was a railroad.
Now it's done.

BIBLIOGRAPHY

Elwood, W. & Bick, P. (1988). *The Milwaukee road*. (monograph). Harlowton, MT: Harlowton's Historic District.

Johnson, S.W. (1997). *The Milwaukee road revisited*. Moscow, ID: University of Idaho Press.

Koeller, J.M. (1996). *The city of Milwaukee*. Volume 2. Edison, NJ: Morning Sun Books Inc.

Lynch, E. (1990). *The Milwaukee electrics*. In *Rail Fan & Railroad* 9(10):77–81. Newton NJ: Carstens Publications Inc.

——— (1990). *The Milwaukee road west: Ten years gone*. In *Rail Fan & Railroad* 9(10):56–69. Newton NJ: Carstens Publications Inc.

Marvel, B. (1996). *Under Milwaukee wires*. Edison, NJ: Morning Sun Books Inc.

McCarter, S. (1992) *The Milwaukee road in Montana*. Helena, MT: Montana Historical Society Press.

Oxford University Press (1998). *Reference encyclopedia*. Oxford, UK: Oxford University Press.

Pentrex (1996). *The Milwaukee road*. Volume 1: *Electric power on the Milwaukee road*. (video). Pasadena, CA: Pentrex.

——— (1996). *The Milwaukee road*. Volume 2: *Harlowton to Butte*. (video). Pasadena, CA: Pentrex.

——— (1996). *The Milwaukee road*. Volume 3: *The Rocky Mountain division*. (video). Pasadena, CA: Pentrex.

Ploss, T.H. (1998). *Supplemental memoirs to the nation pays again*. Wilmette, IL: Our Publishing Co. Inc.

——— (1991) *The nation pays again: The demise of the Milwaukee road 1928–1986*. (3rd edn.). Chicago, IL: Our Publishing Co. Inc.

Wilkerson, W.H. (1998). *Electric passenger locomotives*. (monograph). Harlowton, MT: *The Times-Clarion*.

———. (1996). *Fifty years of Olympians*. monograph. Harlowton, MT: *The Times-Clarion*.

——— (1995). *The Milwaukee road F class locomotives*. (monograph). Harlowton, MT: *The Times-Clarion*.

——— (1994). *The Milwaukee road S class locomotives*. (monograph). Harlowton, MT: *The Times-Clarion*.

——— (1991). *The Milwaukee road EF-4 Little Joe locomotives*. (monograph). Harlowton, MT: *The Times-Clarion*.

——— (1989). *The Milwaukee road class 2-8-2L locomotives*. (monograph). Harlowton, MT: *The Times-Clarion*.

——— (1986). *The Milwaukee road E57B locomotives*. (monograph). Harlowton, MT: *The Times-Clarion*.

York, T. (1987). *North America's great railroads*. Greenwich, CT: Barnes and Noble.

Other Sources:

* The letter quoted in Chapter 12 was written by Charles Goodnow in 1915, a year after electric service was introduced.

Museums Visited:

Charles M. Bair Family Museum, Martinsdale, MT
Musselshell Valley Museum, Harlowton, MT
Powell County Museum, Deer Lodge, MT
Railway Museum, Alberton, MT
Rosebud County Pioneer Museum, Forsyth, MT
Treasure County Museum, Hysham, MT
Virginia City Station and Museum, Virginia City, MT

ABOUT THE AUTHOR

PETER W. ELKINGTON has been described as chronicler, a teller of tales. He comes from a long line of storytellers. His grandmother, and her mother before her, would have the grandchildren gather around for a story hour in the evening. His mother, Katharine, was an extraordinary storyteller. She told tales, some true, some fictitious, that were both vivid and realistic. Peter W. Elkington has continued this tradition by writing and telling stories based on historical events or happenings, or sheer fiction.

Peter lives in Revelstoke, British Columbia. *Once There Was A Railroad* is his sixth book and his fifth volume of fiction. During the summer months he travels widely, gathering new material for his next collection.

Other Books by Peter W. Elkington

FICTION

The Road 1994
The Road West 1995
The Roots of the Road 1997

PHILOSOPHY

We Shall Overcome 1996

BIOGRAPHY

Katharine Wistar Elkinton 2001